REGI'S GODDESS: GODS OF MISFORTUNE 2

Lyn Gala

Chapter One

What are you doing? That is a closed system. Don't open that!" Ter's voice echoed down the metal corridors of the pirate ship the crew had confiscated. Damage to the drive system had grounded the ship on a Kowri planet, but Ter had chosen to disregard the precarious political situation. He was not alone in that.

Captain Cota was using their time on a restricted planet to argue that the Kowri Empire should work with the Coalition. He hadn't used the words "join the Coalition." Yet. However, Regi could hear it hovering in the air on the rare occasion that Kowri exalteds walked slowly enough past the ship that Captain Cota could direct his words in their general direction.

Since the Kowri Empire was technologically advanced and distrustful of outsiders, the Empire was unlikely to appreciate the suggestion. But Cota believed he could convince them otherwise. Worse, he believed that Regi, the lone Kowri to ever leave the Empire to serve on a Coalition ship, had the power to drag exalteds back to the ship to listen to Cota.

At least he had the sense to show caution. Given that Kowri often assumed anyone intruding on their space hoped to steal from them and disrespect Kowri gods, the Empire had a policy of destroying others' ships. That limited how hard Cota was willing to press his agenda.

Ter, on the other hand, was determined to prove he was not intimidated. He was equally happy offending Kowri as any of the hundred or so species making up the Coalition. But the Kowri were not crew members obligated to listen to Ter's complaining. Regi feared that his people would lose patience before Ter ran out of insults.

Regi walked a little faster.

"Wait. How did..." Ter paused, and then his voice increased in volume. "Explain that!" He sounded like a child demanding candy, a comparison Regi did not intend to share since Ter had lived at least a couple of centuries, far longer than the gods had allotted to any Kowri. Regi crossed the threshold, his stomach churning. He'd walked this part of the ship dozens of times since Ter's people had cleared the radiation, but he could not escape the echoes of fear.

Two weeks ago, Regi had been sure he would die—he and Dante. The last pirate had taken refuge here, trusting deadly radiation to keep others out. But Dante had decided to cast his life to the gods and chase the pirate down before he could destroy the ship. The huuman Dante either had remarkable faith or a lack of intelligence, because he had followed Regi into the radiation zone.

Regi could not decide which event was more improbable—a former slave risking his life to save a relative stranger or Divashi, goddess of poisons, saving them both.

Regi entered the room to find two Kowri engineers who looked caught between frustration and homicidal fury. "I have no obligation to explain science to lesser beings," one snapped. Ter puffed out his chest, but his species was slender enough that no amount of posturing would make him the physical equal to a Kowri, even if he had the advantage of height.

"Ter." Regi acknowledged his crew member before turning to the Kowri engineers. "Merbol, Hrole." He touched his temples in greeting. After two weeks back on one of the Kowri worlds, he found the manners of his youth had returned.

"Exalted," Merbol said.

"Hey, Regi." Dante was sitting on a cooling pipe, perched high above the others. He swung his legs slowly as through listening to some music inaudible to the rest of them.

"Dante, I had not known you were here."

"Ter offered to explain ship engines in a way that even idiots could understand, but then these two showed up." Dante's expression had a touch of merriment.

"We are attempting to hurry the repairs," Merbol said. He then gave Ter a narrow-eyed glare. "However, this one slows our work."

"This one," Ter said, spitting the words out, "needs to know how you are isolating the rapid-decay particles."

Nothing could anger Ter faster than having others refuse to explain themselves; however, the Empire would not bow to his preferences. Regi intervened before the situation could grow more volatile. "I doubt they can explain how Kowri developed the process, and they are not allowed to explain the application." The Empire guarded their technology jealously, a trait that inspired their storied history of destroying Coalition ships attempting to approach their worlds.

The only reason the Kowri had not already destroyed this ship and all in it was because a god had noticed Regi. That had forced the temple to offer reluctant assistance. Regi's goddess had caused their Coalition ship to fall into a black hole, so Regi thought the Kowri had an obligation to fix the pirate ship the crew had commandeered. Others debated that issue at some length.

Ter thrust his elbows out at awkward angles. "I'm in charge of these engines. How can I know if they are following safety protocols if I don't understand the process?" Regi tried to reassure him, but Ter continued. "After all, these Empire people are stupid enough to believe a god will save them from their own mistakes. If you allow long decay particles to contaminate the working area, no god will be enough to protect from the cellular damage."

All Regi's sympathy vanished. "Kowri do not rely on the gods." The gods were too capricious for any sane Kowri to leave his fate in their oversized hands. But the implication the gods were not real was too much to bear.

Merbol and Hrole both glared at Ter. Regi had once resented being the only Kowri on a ship full of Coalition members. He had not understood how having additional Kowri in the immediate vicinity would exacerbate his unhappiness. He disliked having the engineers witness his conflict with Ter.

"Since the Lady Divashi chose to protect me from radiation, I maintain that a god is enough to provide protection. That said, we do not expect the gods to take such direct action on our behalf," he said coldly.

"This is not a place for you, exalted." Merbol held his hands low in apology. That was universal Kowri-speak for Please-go-away-so-the-gods-do-not-see-what-we-are-about-to-do. Since the gods were so much larger than corporeal life, they could no more perceive Merbol or Ter or Hrole than the average Kowri could see ants crawling through the fallen leaves of harvest season. However, Regi had her attention. Regi cast a light upon his life, and his goddess could use that to perceive those around him. Since gods often chose to assist their exalteds by gracing them with bad luck to guide their lives toward a favorable outcome, that posed a certain danger.

Furthermore, his goddess had few exalteds. The Lord of justice—Gavd— had thousands upon thousands of chosen ones, and even a god could not see all Kowri space at once. Regi suspected other Kowri feared him not only because his goddess was associated with poison, disorder and her sacred dops, but also because she had so few exalteds. Anyone near Regi might gain the undivided attention of a god.

"Play nice, Ter," Dante said with humor in his voice. Regi realized Ter was muttering invectives under his breath.

Ter poked a pair of long fingers in Dante's direction. "You are free to leave."

"Exalted," Merbol lowered his hands even more, "this is not a proper place for one such as you."

Dante swung his legs faster. "Yeah, if you stay here, you might have to testify against Larry and Moe when they shove Ter headfirst into the engine."

Ter glared at Dante, but Regi suspected Dante had great insight on the conflict, although the translation matrix must have gone terribly wrong for Dante to believe the engineers were named Larry and Moe.

"Do you accuse us of violence?" Hrole demanded. He sounded far more aggravated about Dante's joke than he had about Ter's irreverence. Then again, Kowri did not expect outsiders to respect their gods.

"Nope." Dante held his hands up in a way that Regi associated with his use of humor; however, the two engineers shot to their feet, their hands up in defensive positions. Regi walked between and caught Dante's nearest hand, pulling it down.

"To raise your hand is a signal to begin conflict," he explained. That was as close to a universal gesture as he had seen, but Dante's people assigned a different meaning to it.

"Sorry about that." Dante shifted his hands to show them palm down and low—another near-universal signal. The fact he had picked up on the body language the rest of them used showed his adaptability and intelligence, even if his people appeared to have customs at odds with the rest of the universe. "I am not interested in starting a fight."

Regi turned to face the engineers. "Dante's are a young people who had not encountered another species before he was taken by pirates. He did not intend to threaten anyone. His gesture was one of humor."

"Surrender," Dante said.

Regi frowned at him.

Dante put his hands back up. "We do this to show we don't carry weapons. It's a gesture of surrender meaning we don't want to fight. Although, I do tend to use it when I'm joking, so you aren't wrong about that. But I apologize for making you feel unsafe." He slid down off the pipe. "I should probably avoid shit-stirring around new people."

A horrified silence fell over the small group. Regi was unsure about Dante's motivation in reminding them that he had been a slave often assigned to move excrement and do other distasteful and dangerous work. Perhaps he used the statement to remind the rest of them that their squabbles were petty. Regi agreed on that point.

Ter recovered first. "How does that isotope isolator work?" He closed the distance between himself and Merbol.

Merbol brought his hands up. "I begin to think the huuman's suggestion has merit."

"It does not," Regi said sharply. "If you cannot work under Ter's direction, then the temple will have to sacrifice efficiency and allow Ter to repair the engine without assistance." Merbol's mouth opened, no doubt to lodge a protest, but Regi turned to Ter. "And if you wish for assistance and access to Kowri technology, the price you must pay is patience. They deserve to work without interrogation." Regi looked from Ter to the Kowri engineers and back. "So, Ter, do these two have permission to work on the engines?" Regi could not predict Ter's behavior. The man was short-tempered and demanding, but much of his poor behavior was motivated by a deep sense of obligation to protect the crew.

After a moment, Ter let his arms hang at his sides. "If they do something that makes the engines overload, I will spend endless days detailing the breadth and width of your stupidity in painful detail."

"If we fail, the reaction will lead to our deaths, so you will have to speak quickly," Merbol snapped. This was going as well as Regi had expected.

"You're the ones who believe in multiple lives," Ter said. "I will find you in the next one. Isolate the radiation to the far side of the chamber and I'll navigate the repair bot." Turning, Ter dropped into the chair attached to the control panel. The conversation was over from his point of view. Merbol stared balefully at the back of Ter's head for a moment before he returned to the Kowri equipment. Hrole gifted Ter with an obscene gesture before he did the same.

"I should get back to the dops." Dante moved toward the door with silent steps.

Regi still had trouble believing pirates had farmed the sacred dops for their poisonous quills, using the fast-action paralytic as the main ingredient in a new recreational drug with soporific and hallucinogenic properties. The work required them to steal slaves since no sane criminal would handle such dangerous animals. In contrast, Dante handled dops as easily as a parent handled an infant—with care but also with great affection.

His habit of spending so much time in the room where the last of the dops lived worried Regi. It worried Ean as well, but Dante refused to speak with her despite her expertise in assisting individuals who had suffered trauma.

"You could explore," Regi said.

Dante gave him an incredulous look. "I've scrubbed every inch of this ship, usually with some pirate standing six feet behind me barking orders. I'll stick with Peaches."

Peaches. Dante had named the dominant female dop—a creature with enough poison to kill ten men—using a name associated with sweet tree-grown fruit. Regi wondered if the mental deficiencies were a symptom of distress or if huumans suffered some lack of logic.

"I have to make it up to her that I left her without food and water for three days," Dante said. "I still can't believe you idiots couldn't find a concealed door."

"The pirates were experts at concealing them." Despite his words, Regi did feel guilt. Had Dante not chanced upon a temple dop and asked about those on the ship, the animals might have died in their hidden prison. Given the creatures were sacred to Divashi, that would have brought the goddess's ire down on someone. The pirates who had been on the ship when Regi's crew had taken it were dead and the other members of the crew were hidden in Coalition space, so Regi feared the crew might have paid for the oversight.

Dante snorted and headed into the corridor. "Maybe I had too high expectations for my first aliens, but I would think you would notice that there was a great chunk of the deck inaccessible from any direction, which would have led you to suspect a door."

"Lady Onidba, goddess of logic, would agree," Regi admitted.

Dante's voice dropped to a deeper pitch. "Still, feeding the hedgehogs was my job."

"Dops," Regi corrected him. If Lady Divashi watched, Regi did not wish for Dante to offer offence by misnaming her sacred creatures.

Dante stopped at the top of a ladder set at an awkward angle. The curved bottom of the Coalition ship was designed for a dock sling, but the Kowri had none. It left the entire ship tilting uncomfortably. Perhaps that was part of the reason for the crew's restlessness. Either that or they suspected the truth of the temple debates around the Coalition ship and crew. Regi hoped not. They did not deserve to live in fear that the negotiations were in danger of failing.

"Dops... poisonous hedgehogs... *poTAEto... poTAHto.*"

Regi frowned, not following any of that response.

Dante sighed. "I owe Peaches. She's getting on in years, and she needs the company."

"Other dops have stayed. If she were lonely, she would leave when we open the doors for her." They still did so regularly; Exalted Nawr kept requesting it. Nawr had been the most fair-minded of the exalteds so far, not taking a position as much as listening to all sides and seeking more information. He embraced his roles as senior exalted and the chosen of Ectipic, Goddess of protection. He did not press for any vote in the temple, which maintained the safety of the Coalition crew, but Regi feared that the crew's nerves would lead someone to make a fatal error if they continued to be trapped in a stolen pirate ship with hundreds of Kowri weapons pointed at them.

"You may believe Lady Divashi guides Peaches," Dante touched his forehead as he named the goddess, a gesture uniquely huuman but one of respect, "but I think it's more likely the old lady was born in captivity and doesn't know what to do with herself outside that room."

Regi winced. To question the movements of a sacred animal was to question the gods. Perhaps Dante's words were a sign from the Lady Divashi that he should not involve Dante in issues of temple politics. After all, if Regi held him out as a theologically acceptable outsider and Dante failed in that role, it could prove more disastrous than all Ter's yelling. The Kowri expected poor behavior from one who called the gods imaginary.

However, the gods did not move that way. They did not give ambiguous signs or cause individuals to speak with their voices. Regi's case of broken ribs was far more typical of the assistance gods provided. Bad luck was the first gift of the gods, after all. More firm in his path, he asked Dante, "Can I speak with you privately?"

Dante frowned, a gesture where he lowered the fur over his eyes. "Um, sure," he said. "We can talk in my room." He had laid out blankets and pillows on a shipping cushion so he could sleep in the room where the pirates had kept the dop cages. Sadly, that was an improvement over his insistence that he sleep in the converted cargo hold that had been the slave quarters. It scared Regi that the lives of the crew might rest on the abilities of someone who was so damaged. He had to trust that his goddess had a plan. And he did. Lady Divashi could guide him in all things. He just worried that the lives of a Coalition crew would be so small in her sight that she might not notice when those lives were ended.

Chapter Two

Dante led the way back to the room he'd claimed. With the ship at such an uncomfortable angle, the bunks in his old room were likely to dump him out of bed when he rolled over. Besides, the smell of the dops was comforting. The pirates wanted poison from the dops' quills, but the tiny creatures were a source of terror for them. They had avoided the room, so it had become Dante's only refuge.

Regi followed Dante into the room and closed the door behind him. He then stood with an expression that hinted at severe constipation. The Kowri were handsome people with strong features and black and gray tiger stripes, but they lacked a certain alienness that Dante saw in the others. In low light, Dante could imagine Regi was human. Ter resembled a poorly assembled scarecrow and Regi's security assistant had a nose that looked like a mole and an elephant had had a baby and stuck its nose in the middle of a baboon's face. Not attractive. The doctor had boobs running all down a body wide enough to make a sumo wrestler envious, and the psychologist they kept foisting on him resembled a shuffling pyramid with a neck larger than her head and four stubby legs that seemed incapable of carrying out the task of lifting her mass.

But Kowri had soulful eyes and familiar faces. Their velvet fur and the extra thumb on the outside of their hand were odd, but not disturbing. But despite all that attractiveness, the species was so xenophobic that they would destroy ships rather than risk having aliens spy on them.

Dante trusted Regi, but he had chosen to leave his people. He had abandoned his grand Empire with their temples and their gods and had fled to the Coalition. While Dante could believe that Regi was a good man, he had trouble believing the same for the other Kowri. And seeing as how the ship was broken and stranded on a Kowri world, that thought was not a comfort.

"I have a request." Regi lifted his hands halfway to his temples before lowering them again. Dante had seen the gesture often enough to suspect it was his version of crossing himself, the way Dante's Catholic grandmother had every time someone mentioned Dante's father. He didn't know if his grandmother was asking for forgiveness for whatever murderous thoughts she harbored for her son-in-law or if she was praying for her daughter to leave the bastard, but Regi's gesture had the same solemn element of ritual. Since Kowri gods took a more active role in life, Dante could appreciate the need to avoid pissing off such powerful, non-corporeal neighbors.

"Anything." Dante owed Regi his freedom and his life. Dante had been considering ways to make the pirates kill him when Regi had spotted the pirate ship hiding at the edge of a black hole. Dante might have taken a page from Carlos and angered one of the dops before jamming a hand down on it, but the pain Carlos had suffered was more than Dante could bear. His whole hand had swollen, before the writhing and screaming and vomiting of blood started. Dante had reached a point where he wished for death, but he was a coward when it came to pain.

"I am called to the temple." Regi wrinkled his nose in an expression of disgust.

"I hope you are better at concealing your emotions when you are in front of your temple leaders."

Regi laughed, a huge honking noise that still startled Dante if he wasn't prepared for it. "I grew up the only child of a temple exalted. I assure you I know how to avoid being impolitic."

"I hope so, seeing as how your people appear to hold all the cards in this situation."

"To which cards do you refer?" Regi asked, tilting his head to the side in confusion. The gesture made him cute—a term he would likely not appreciate. The man was a security chief, after all.

"I mean that your people seem to have all the power here since the Coalition ship is still disabled."

Regi scratched the side of his neck. "There is some debate on whether this ship is rightfully belongs to the Coalition."

A rock formed in Dante's gut. If the Kowri took the ship away from this crew, where would the crew go? Dante had a few theories, but none he wished to say aloud. "Why?"

"Certain exalteds argue that the Lady Divashi led me to the ship in order to save her sacred dops." Regi cast an uneasy look at the male dop sitting on the top of Regi's boot and clinging to his pant leg. Dante would have rescued Regi, but in the past, the smaller males had leapt out of Dante's hand to land on Regi's shoulder or head. Regi always flinched away from that, so Dante left the small male to molest Regi's ankle in peace.

"Maybe it's because I'm human and we don't have a lot of experience in space seeing as how we only have two planets and mostly fly back and forth between the two, but it does seem like the captain of the crew would pull rank on a security officer. That would make Captain Cota the one in charge of the ship."

"Captain Cota will, no doubt, make that very argument when this debate reaches his ears. However, Leevshi and Bekdi are exceptionally vocal in wanting to claim the ship and both are disturbingly silent on what should happen to the crew."

"Leevshi? Which one is he?" Dante asked. He had always disparaged his father and his political ambitions, but his old man had an uncanny ability to make political alliances. Dante was trying to emulate his father and get a sense of where the political fault lines were among these temple exalteds.

The only thing it had taken to get him to respect any part of his father's life was an alien kidnapping and several months of captivity where he watched everyone who had been taken with him die one after another. He suspected that was a rather pointed example of irony.

"Leevshi is the follower of Dicia, the God of crystals."

Some of the temple associations helped Dante understand personalities. Nawr was a follower of Ectipic, and that goddess of protection certainly did seem to rub off on him. He had insisted that the Coalition crew remain safe in the ship, and even unquestioned as long as the temple debated. But Dante could not imagine what being a follower of the God of crystals would say about someone's personality. "Crystals?"

Regi drew his mouth into a pucker. "He is young and as brittle as a crystal. I tend to think of the exalteds of Dicia as being insightful and perhaps a little inflexible in their thinking, but this debate has proved unsettling for Leevshi."

"Wait. Is he the one who stormed out of the meeting last week?"

"Yes, but I am not overly concerned about Leevshi. He may be an exalted, but he is young and intemperate. The others are unlikely to be swayed by his more martial suggestions. I am far more concerned about Bekdi."

Dante knew that name. "He is the follower of Gavd, God of justice, isn't he?"

"He is."

The man was taller than Dante, and Dante had a good eight to twelve inches on most of the Kowri. He was the Kowri equivalent of a police officer, a comparison that made Dante deeply uncomfortable. A gay man in Texas had few reasons to trust the police. "He looks like he would win a fistfight."

"I'd do not understand the reference to fighting with one's fists. I assure you, the temple does not solve disputes that way."

Dante huffed. "No, I mean he's large. He's a real bruiser."

"Regi nodded before bringing his hands together and touching his four thumbs in a diamond shape in front of his chest. "He is a da-male, and they are larger. While everyone chooses his or her own path, da-males are typically seen as being slower to anger and more rational. Bekdi is old enough that his words carry weight. Where he goes Nuruti follows."

All the names were giving Dante a headache. At least Regi had given up trying to use their full temple-name, which involved the exalted, their god, their mother's name and her god, and the names of their two fathers. It was a lot. However, even without being able to place all the individuals, Dante got the general idea. "You're saying that the temple debates are going against us."

"They do not appear in our favor. But it is to our advantage that the Lady Divashi stands firmly by my side." Regi knelt slowly and put his hand on the deck palm up to allow the dop to crawl into it. The creature used his tiny paws to grip Regi's inner thumb. "Where the gods lead, even reluctant Kowri must follow. And we are not entirely without supporters. I came to ask you to come with me to the temple to meet with Sibja and Alb. They appear most likely to support our claim that the Lady Divashi sees not only me but also the Coalition crew."

"So that's two against four firm supporters of the kill-the-infidels position?" Those sounded like less than favorable odds, and it left dozens if not hundreds of Kowri exalteds avoiding the debate. Dante's father had always said that winning a political fight was about getting the opposition to stay home more than in turning out numbers on your own side. After years... hell, decades... of ignoring his father's advice, Dante wished he had listened more often.

Regi winced. "Nuruti is not advocating violence."

"But you said he follows where Bekdi leads, and Bekdi seems pretty unforgiving." Dante wondered if that was a universal trait for all the followers of Gavd. Dante had not met many Kowri, but the followers of that god all seemed like unforgiving bastards.

"Bekdi would not put Gavd up against Divashi, and I have great hope that Alb can convince some of the silent exalteds to take our side. She has a way of convincing others."

Regi had mentioned that name before. She was a follower of Oba, the Lady of writing, and so old that she was nearly white. Dante had seen her from a distance and had thought for a moment that she was albino.

"And who does Sibja follow?" Dante needed a flow chart, but that was true for human politics as well. That was why he preferred the back of a horse. Give him a dozen city people who had horse riding on their bucket list any day of the week. He'd rather deal with entitlement and ignorance than politics.

"Iloxot, Lady of punishment."

Dante winced. "Well, I guess I would rather have that lady support us than not." Dante sat on the edge of the straw bin someone had dragged in as a sort of offering to the dops. "Regi, be honest. What are the odds that your people will let us off this planet or even let us live?"

Regi settled on the edge of the bed Dante had made for himself. The awkward angle of the floor meant he squatted awkwardly for a minute before he gave in to gravity and leaned back against the wall. "My people will not kill you. There is no version of justice that would justify it."

"Not even if Ter keeps demanding access to Kowri technology?"

Again, Regi grimaced. Dante suspected their situation was more dire than Regi was willing to admit, but after spending months as a slave, Dante's fear seemed almost inaccessible. It was as if he had faced death for so long that it was a foregone conclusion and all he could control was the amount of pain he might suffer on his journey there. Dante suspected this was not a healthy point of view, which might explain why the mountainous Ean kept asking him to explicate his feelings. The translator needed work, but Dante could spot a psychologist, even in an alien body.

"I will admit, it would be easy for the Kowri to strand us here," Regi said softly. "But the Lady left me no choice when she continued to damage the ship. I had to bring us here or risk dying in space when the goddess pushed too hard for flesh to survive her attempt to assist us."

"I don't blame you," Dante hurried to say. He should have anticipated the guilt, but he hadn't. The Lady Divashi had forced them to land here. Maybe the Coalition crew dismissed her as a figment of Kowri imagination, but Dante believed. He wasn't sure she was a god, and he knew she wasn't *the* God, but she had mighty god-like hands and too little understanding of the fragility of life. "They could turn this ship into a prison that would hold us for the rest of our natural lives."

"Given how long Bevti's and Ter's species lives, that would be awkward."

Dante noticed that was not a denial.

"However," Regi said with more cheer, "I want you to come with me today to speak with Alb and Sibja. They need to see that outsiders can be respectful of the gods and maybe then they will believe that the gods can respect outsiders."

"Me? I'm not even a member of the Coalition. I'm a nobody from a species so unimportant that none of you has ever heard of us."

"And that would be in our favor as well. I know it has been a millennium since the Coalition feigned broken navigation systems and overheating engines to justify crossing the Kowri border, but Kowri adore history and possess an unwillingness to forget insults. The fact that you are not Coalition will work in your favor as will your lack of avarice around Kowri technology. Ter's technological envy and Cota's political machinations are dangerous. I fear those two would simply reinforce every stereotype that the exalteds hold of the Coalition."

"So what? I make nice with the two gentlemen in the hope that they can talk a host of exalteds into siding with us?" That seemed dangerously optimistic. Dante wasn't skilled with words, even when everyone spoke English. Add in the odd phrasing and missing words of the implanted translator and Dante was almost sure he was a menace, rhetorically speaking.

"Sibja and Alb are both female, as is our other strong supporter, Gimi, but I am hoping we can speak with her later. Gimi is a follower of Onidba, Lady of logic, and she tends to ask so many questions and challenge her own beliefs to such an extent that she makes others question everything they believed. If we are meeting with those who support us, she is best excluded. Most find the followers of Onidba disquieting in conversation.

"Sounds like some lawyers I know." Like his father. "So three on our side, and you're hoping I can give the two ladies some ammunition they can use to convince the others."

"I am. The majority of exalteds remain neutral in this matter, waiting for some god to provide a sign. But I fear that sometimes my people wait too long for the gods, even when we know that they rarely intervene in our worlds. I know you have had a strange introduction to Kowri, but we are inclined to lead boring lives. The gods intervene in most Kowri's lives only once or twice, thank the host of the heavens." Regi rubbed his own ribs where they had been broken. Regi often said that the first gift of a god was bad luck, so hopefully the Kowri would reach some reasonable conclusion before any of these great beings felt the need to stick oversized fingers into this mess. Dante had thought politics back home was difficult but knowing that powerful creatures watched ready to rain down bad luck if a person chose wrong was a new level of misery, one that even his father would not appreciate.

"Will me talking to them help?" Dante asked. "I can't tell them anything important about the Coalition or soothe any of their fears, especially since it sounds pretty reasonable to fear that Coalition folks might steal their technology."

"I hope you can help." Regi did not sound convinced. But sometimes when a man had only poor choices in front of him, he had to choose the lesser of the evils. Dante's SAT tutor had said something similar. If all the answers were wrong, choose the least wrong option. That seemed a stupid way to earn a spot in a university, but much of life seemed stupid to Dante. If Regi said this was the least wrong option, Dante believed him.

He stood. "Well then, let's go talk to these ladies of yours and convince them that I am not the barbarian they seem to assume."

Chapter Three

Dante took a deep breath of fresh air as he stepped into the air. Walking around the pirate ship was the only exercise the authorities allowed, so he had indulged at least once a day. After months locked inside small rooms and stuffy corridors, he needed time in the fresh air, and so he'd grown used to Kowri stares when he left the safety of the hull. Safety. He never thought he'd apply that word to the pirate ship.

Compared to the narrow rockets that travelled between Earth and Mars, the pirate ship was a luxury liner of infinite size. Compared to the Gavd vessels, it was a bug upturned on its rounded back, surrounded by coyotes that could snap it up at any time. Dante had no idea why anyone would need such huge vessels, but given how territorial Kowri were about their technology, Dante had chosen to keep his questions to himself.

Instead of leading them in a circle for exercise, Regi led them toward the closest temple, a white stone building with a bluish tint. Dante gave him a sidelong look. The last time Dante had approached the temple, a dozen different Kowri had almost broken their necks trying to block the entrance before Dante could do anything as horrifying as step foot in the sacred space. Dante had a friend who was Mormon who felt the same about non-believers going into the temple. Being raised Baptist, Dante didn't quite understand, but he had been raised to be a polite guest, and he was even more committed to that when the hosts owned heavy weaponry.

"Are we visiting the temple?" Dante asked.

Regi pressed the back of his fingers to his temples. Definitely sacrilegious. "Alb has an office near the pronaos."

"The what?"

"The area in front of the temple where the side walls shield the cobbled pathway," Regi answered.

"So... entrance?" Dante asked. The translator had provided pronaos when Regi's original word had contained more growling sounds, so Dante assumed the word was English, but Richard had corrupted the translation program. Before he'd taken up a career as a dop-tending slave who taught improvisational shuffleboard, he'd been a history professor. There were times he was the only one who understood the strange vocabulary that came out of the program. Dante had an associate degree in Equine Science, but he had never taken to college or the vocabulary that came with it. He could recognize a healthy coronet band or diagnose *Streptococcus equi*, but he didn't have much of a formal education.

"Yes," Regi said. "Alb's vocation means that she meets many petitioners, not all of whom are comfortable in the cold weather temple. Even Kowri fear the animals sacred to the cold-weather gods."

Dante assumed that was another veiled suggestion that his fondness for dops made him strange. Knowing he was as out-of-place among the Kowri as he had been in Texas, he worried. He had to impress two women, and that had never been his forte. He assumed that Alb a'Oba would have more sway because of her age. In his family, even when the men were at their misogynistic best, no one ever contradicted his grandmother.

A large Kowri stood in the shadow of the temple entrance, watching as they veered to one side. This part of the sidewalk was empty—only trees rustling overhead in the lazy wind made any sound. Dante would call it a perfect day, but the stares of the Kowri on the main walk behind him still bored into his back. The path followed the curve of the temple, giving the illusion they were alone. "What exactly does an exalted of writing do?" Dante asked, more to distract himself than out of any curiosity about what an alien priestess might have on her agenda.

"Largely, she writes," Regi said without an ounce of sarcasm.

Dante blinked, waiting for the follow up joke, but it didn't come. "I had guessed that much. But on my world, there are different forms of writing. A person might make up fiction stories or write about news events." Dante would remember more genres if he were a reader. But in his defense, his childhood consisted of trying to escape the house, which meant on horseback, and horseback was not a great place for reading.

"An exalted of Oba might write in any format, but he or she has written so well that the goddess has noticed. However, their most sacred duty comes at death."

"That sounds vaguely morbid. What can they do at death?" Dante braced himself, half prepared to hear some tale worthy of a horror movie.

"Over the course of a lifetime, the exalted will be sought out by many who wish for their stories to be told. The exalted writes each one, sometimes even using a person's own words as if stepping into that person's life. Those writings are sacred and kept in close confidence until the exalted dies. Then all their sacred writings are published and millions of Kowri will have access to life stories that would otherwise pass into obscurity. For the common Kowri who attempt to stay as far away from the gods as they can, that is seen as a form of immortality."

"Do your people doubt that the soul is immortal?" Dante always felt as though something happened after a person died. If not, then the universe put a lot of effort into teaching people only to throw those lessons away at the point of death.

"My people are unsure. Do huumans believe in the afterlife?"

Dante smiled at Regi's attempt to emulate a Texas drawl every time he said *human*. "Most do. Plenty are unsure, and some are firmly convinced that death is the end. Mostly I figure I'm not smart enough to know the truth, so I stay out of the debate." Up until Dante had announced his sexual orientation, his agnosticism had been the family scandal. "Are the writings always held in confidence? What if someone describes a murder he committed or wants to commit? What if someone brags about all the plans he's put in place to kill his wife?"

Regi's discomfort was clear in his expression. After a long pause, he said, "We must trust the gods to sort such matters."

Dante didn't trust that answer when it came from priests, and he didn't when it came from aliens. "You yourself said that the gods are so large that seeing an individual Kowri is like trying to spot a grain of sand."

"It would be closer to a pebble. After all, the gods can perceive us and our differences as we can differentiate hues and shapes of pebbles if we focus our attention."

Dante imagined enormous creatures on their hands and knees, staring down into the world until they could differentiate a Regi-shaped pebble from a Dante-shaped one. "The gods must have some bad backs," he muttered before taking a breath. "The gods will not intervene if a Kowri-shaped pebble shares a murder plot. Doesn't that mean that the exalted have an obligation to do it instead?"

"You assume that the gods have no ability to mediate such a conflict, but I assure you, they can. More than one exalted who had taken a story of particular interest was overcome by more bad luck than he or she could survive. At which point, the writings were made public."

So, the god of writing killed her own priests to make stories public. Perhaps Regi thought that made his people sound reasonable, but it didn't. "What if the gods weren't looking at that pebble at that exact moment? When do exalteds have an obligation to protect an innocent person if they are warned about pending violence?"

Regi touched his temple. "That is not our way." The man was too polite to accuse Dante of being an asshole, but he was probably thinking it.

However, Dante could not control his own disgust. "Your way sucks."

Regi's ears flattened. It was not difficult to interpret that expression. In fact, Dante's horse had leveled that expression at him more than once. And like when his horse had done it, it preceded a sharp kick.

"I don't mean to be disrespectful," Dante said in his most conciliatory tone. He cursed himself for being so fucking incapable of getting control of his own emotions.

"You are disrespecting the gods," Regi said in a factual tone that made the condemnation somehow worse.

Dante took a deep breath. "I lost my mother when I was fairly young." Dante swallowed the emotions that threatened to spill over. He generally refused to talk about his past. At one point, his father had wanted him to trot the family history out for some reporter. His father had learned to regret using Dante in his political machinations.

Regi stopped and studied Dante openly. "I am sorry you had to carry that burden so young. The loss of a parent is a particularly difficult trauma for children to navigate."

"Yeah, it is." Dark laughter bubbled up inside, but Dante swallowed it. If he lost his composure, Regi would call Ean, and Dante could not handle that. "But part of my trauma came from the fact that a priest had good reason to suspect my mother was in danger, and he said nothing."

"What is a priest? That term does not translate."

Dante considered all the ways he could define that term. He could corrupt the damn translation technology with his most creative invective. The temptation was there. "A priest is a type of exalted, only without the government powers. They take confession, which means people tell them the bad things they've done, and the priest is supposed to help them work through those sins and learn to be a better person. Theoretically." In practice, Dante suspected confession was people offloading their guilt so they could go out and be assholes again. He would never express that sentiment in front of his grandmother because, like all proper Southern men, he was terrified of his grandmother. However, he had lost his ability to forgive some sins.

Regi's ears rose. "The translation device is not providing a translation I understand."

Dante snorted. The first time he tried talking to someone about his trauma, his chosen audience couldn't understand. That was a perfect metaphor for his life. "The man who killed my mother had gone to confession. He had told the priest that he was angry that my mother had rejected him. He hated that she had a husband and three children and success while he had nothing." The irony was that he had been jealous of an illusion. Dante's home had been anything but the happy nuclear family they projected to the outside world.

"I assume your exalteds have the same prohibition against sharing divine stories."

"Yeah. But if he had chosen to value life over an obligation to a God who probably doesn't even notice him, my mother would still be alive." The wound was old, but it still festered like abscesses on a cow's hoof.

Regi hesitated before saying, "I feel pity and astonishment."

Dante didn't know how to feel about someone who admitted to the pity. He could read as much in faces when people realized who he was... who his mother had been. However, few admitted it. Dante focused on the second half. "Why are you amazed?"

"I have never read of any culture whose beliefs are so like Kowri. And so, I do understand your anger. In theology classes, we learn that the grand dramas that define our lives are a shadow play for the gods.

We are encouraged to trust the gods but accept that we will never understand them. It is a difficult way to live."

Regi sounded like the psychologists Dante had visited as a kid. None had cured his anger. It hadn't helped that Dante's father had then built a career out of the sympathy he had garnered. His get tough on crime platform was not different than most Texas politicians, but others didn't have the specter of a dead wife and pictures of crying children to bolster their campaigns. Sometimes Dante wondered if his mother wouldn't have been happier if she hadn't stayed a nurse and lived a smaller life.

He cleared his throat. "We're not that similar. My people believe our God sees even the smallest bird in its nest. But the way you keep talking about religion.... You can't tell me that the entire universe is full of atheists except for Kowri."

Regi wrinkled his nose. "There are different cultures and theories about the soul and the afterlife. However, a belief in tangible gods is rare, and even when a vernal society does hold such beliefs, when they begin to travel into space and find not the heavens, but science, that belief falters."

That made sense. Dante's father raged against the loss of traditional beliefs. "My people are in the faltering stage. Some people believe in God, some people believe in different gods, some people believe that there is some great universal force that we can't understand, and more and more people believe that we are the only beings to watch over our own lives."

Regi eased into the shadow of a huge tree with arching branches and red flowers. "Where do you fall?" he asked softly.

Dante had spent his youth railing against religion, which explained his father's willingness to pay for any activities that kept Dante out of the public's eye. However, Regi had earned more honesty. "I am firmly and entirely agnostic."

Regi tilted his head. "That translated as a contradiction. It says that you are unquestioningly, questioning."

Dante laughed. "That seems like a fair interpretation."

Regi studied him, his ears forward. His ears might not have much range, but they did tend to emote effectively.

"I'm not smart enough to understand beings large enough to consider us pebbles, so I admit my ignorance. We don't want to be late." Dante gestured toward the curving path. If he had to meet with a woman who seemed like the closest this planet got to a Catholic priest, Dante needed some time without Regi's knowing gaze on him. He was too sharp, and Dante felt like he was fraying at the edges. Given the other woman was an exalted of Iloxot, which sounded vaguely like a judge, he needed to get his emotions under control.

He had a job. He had to convince these people that outsiders deserved respect. In a lifetime of running away from problems, Dante had never felt such an intense urge to flee. However, he didn't have his horse or a bus pass, or any other forms of retreat he'd used in the past. So, he had to do the one thing he'd always avoided. He had to push through and fix the shit in front of him.

Chapter Four

Regi stopped at a door carved with a darting school of itnbo chasing prey through the water. Those who served Oba required privacy, so this stretch of the road was bordered by temple wall on one side and old trees on the other. The air had a fetid sweetness from the spoiled fruit that had fallen to the dirt at the edge of the stone walk. Newer homes had visitor bells that functioned much like the chimes on a Coalition ship, but this home was old enough that an old bell wheel stood near the entrance. He tugged the wheel, and the headstock swung toward them as the bell swung away.

Alb opened the door immediately, and Regi touched his temples. "Exalted Alb a'Oba," he greeted her. He would have added the rest of her name, but he couldn't remember the names of both her fathers.

"Regi a' Divashi," she greeted him. She turned her body to the side, revealing the second woman. "I introduce Sibja a'Iloxot."

"I introduce Dante a'Texas," Regi offered.

Dante smiled and touched two fingers to the crown of his head. "Howdy."

"Please, enter with the twin blessings of the gods, preferably more of the second than the first," Alb said with a twinkle of mischief in her eye. It was poor manners to ask the gods to provide more opportunity than challenge, but Regi appreciated that only an exalted could appreciate the difficulty of having too much of the gods' first blessing.

Regi followed Alb into a parlor filled with carved figures and textiles and books crowded around a large vid screen. His grandfathers had lived in a house very similar to this, but Regi had lived so long in Coalition space that wood carvings and rugs appeared quaint and out of place in living quarters.

"Dante a'Texas," Sibja said, the first individual to acknowledge Dante's relationship with his god. "You are the one who attends the dops that remain on the outsiders' ship." She settled into a Savonarola chair and studied Dante. She was tall and well-muscled, and she leaned back, displaying her body. Either she was attracted to Dante, attempting to show him that she was physically able to defend herself or Regi had lost the ability to understand his own people's body language. He feared the latter.

"Yes, ma'am," Dante said. He studied the room, clearing his throat and glancing at Regi with some concern. Regi hesitated before lowering himself to a chaise, but he could not interpret Dante's body language with any more confidence than Sibja's. After a second, Dante sat on the other end of the chaise, his gaze sweeping the room in a way that spoke of either discomfort or suspicion. After years of living on the austere Coalition ships, Regi understood his discomfort.

Like all good Kowri, Oba had wood and stone carvings of favorite gods to commemorate specific moments in her lives. She had given them a prominent place next to her vid, including one featuring a freio and a pebafri in a mortal battle, a goddess's clawed hand supporting the combatants. No doubt that had a fascinating story behind it. One should not keep the air inside so warmed or so cooled as to be out of season with the exterior, so she had a cacophony of rugs scattered across the wooden floor. Regi could cite the logical reason for each part of the décor, and yet the pieces were overwhelming for eyes that had grown accustomed to other aesthetics.

Alb settled into a cushioned chair with worn arms. "There are few who would care for the Lady Divashi's sacred creatures. They do have a deadly reputation."

"No one gave me a choice about whether or not to do the attending," Dante said softly, but Regi imagined some condemnation in his tone.

"How horrible," Sibja said. Her fingers tightened on the arms of her chair. She was, no doubt, plotting the punishments she would impose if the pirates were found in the Empire. "I understand the lawbreakers schemed to use dop poison."

"They did," Regi said. "Many cultures use pharmaceuticals to distance themselves from reality or dull pain. We found evidence of a new substance that relied heavily on diluted dop poison."

"Was that the only ship to produce this substance?" Sibja asked. She had dived straight to the deepest of the waters.

"We do not know," Regi admitted. "The Coalition has charged my crew with arresting pirates, so when we can get back to Coalition space, I hope we will be charged with finding any others who might be working with these pirates." Regi's chest ached at the idea of other ships with other slaves and other captured dops. Neither the Coalition nor the Empire could allow this to continue.

Alb growled. "I am horrified. I have never before said this, but those pirates deserve the full attention of the Lady Divashi, and I hope she finds a creative end for them." She touched her temples with the back of her fingers before she focused her gaze on Dante. "If you wish to have your tale recorded, I will devote as much time as required to ensuring that your story is told well. I don't know if Regi has explained the obligations of those who follow the Lady Oba, but I do consider it a sacred duty to ensure that unusual stories such as yours are recorded for history."

"I appreciate that," Dante said, but something in the stiffness of his shoulders suggested that he had no intention of ever agreeing to Alb's request. Dante trusted Regi with his truth, but he had no trust for someone as respected as Alb a'Oba.

That could be a problem. Lady Oba's exalteds were judged by the quality of the stories they left behind just as the followers of Gavd were judged by the lawbreakers they were able to bring to justice. His story would enrich Alb's private library, and any rejection could turn her away from their cause.

Regi wondered what the exalteds of Lady Divashi were judged by. Theology class had not covered her history in any detail, but he hoped no one expected him to poison any public figures. That was her most historically significant task.

Alb peered at Dante, her eyes pale with age. "Exalted Regi a'Divashi suggests your people are respectful of the gods."

"Not exactly," Dante said.

Regi's guts curled into a tight ball, and he cursed himself for not better preparing Dante for these questions. However, he had worried that if Dante presented himself as rehearsed and formal, his story would be unconvincing. Perhaps Regi had put too much faith in Dante's piety, though.

"Can you elaborate?" Alb asked.

"Different groups have different belief systems, so we're not quite as unified as Kowri with their single pantheon."

Alb chuckled and Sibja gave her an amused look. "Perhaps Regi has been overly generous in describing our people," Sibja said, "or perhaps he was simply young and naïve when he left the Empire, but I assure you that we are rarely unified in anything."

"That's a little reassuring. I was starting to think my people were coming off as cantankerous in comparison. So are there Kowri who don't believe in Gavd and Divashi and the others?" Dante's pronunciations of the divine names had improved over the last week.

Alb wrinkled her nose. "I believe the translator is malfunctioning. What does belief have to do with the existence of Gavd or Divashi?"

Dante glanced over to Regi, and Regi spread his hand, inviting Dante to continue. These two needed to see the size and scope of outsider belief. Only then could they present to others both the differences and the striking similarities.

Dante cleared his throat. "Among my people, some believe very strongly in one God some worship another or even a group of gods or Buddha, which I don't quite understand. But they see God's fingerprints on their life. But others dismiss that belief as superstition and see that same god-touch as nothing more than luck. We tend to associate good luck with God more than you folks seeing as how bad luck is the first gift of your gods."

Sibja opened her mouth and closed it without speaking. Alb found her voice first. "There is much confusion about which luck is inspired by the gods and which is inspired by a lack of watching where one walks on an uneven path," she said slowly, as if feeling her way around the words. "However, the existence of the gods is undeniable. One can scan an individual to determine whether the gods' energy is present."

"My people don't have that," Dante said. "We are significantly behind the Coalition in technology, and the Coalition appears to be significantly behind you. I'm pretty sure that means we're at the back of this horse race."

Ignoring the illogical reference to huuman horses, Regi said, "At one point, our people used the temple challenge because we had no other way to determine who might be touched by a god." Regi turned his attention to Alb. "I suspect that Dante's people are less like us today and more like what our people were when we lived on only two or three planets."

"That would suggest that his people are exceptionally young and likely foolish. Our people were." Alb's voice had a dreamlike quality, and her gaze grew unfocused as she was lost in some memory, perhaps of a tale from one of those ancient adventurers who revered the Lady Poque above all.

"I would not disagree with that, ma'am."

Sibja pounced on that wording. "Does that imply that you agree that your people are foolish?"

"It means I don't have enough evidence, and I don't want to be forced into arguing for a side when I don't know the truth. So, I am choosing to remain silent."

Alb laughed, and Dante jerked as if the loud sound startled him. "If you have sense enough to say that, then your people are less foolish than Kowri were at that point in our development."

"Then what do you mean by saying that your people are not as united as Regi implied?"

Alb looked to Sibja, but she had a sour expression on her face. That expression revealed the direction of her thoughts, and Regi's stomach soured. "The heretics," Regi said. He had read of them, but it was not a topic for polite conversation, and he did not want the exalteds to associate huuman diversity of belief with the heresies, so he would rather avoid the topic. If Kowri believed huumans lived in a way that emulated the bad behavior of such rogues, the exalteds would move against Dante.

Chapter Five

Alb filled the uneasy silence. "All gods are equal, but certain heretics do enjoy exalting one god or a small cadre of gods above others. The followers of Gavd are rabid in their respect for all gods because the god of justice would accept nothing less. But among those who have been rejected from Gavd's service, there are those who believe that the god of justice is more significant and should be given more respect than other gods. The Lady Jinja, goddess of the unknowable, is sometimes upheld as the most revered, and others believe Retav, Lord of retribution is the primary god."

"Others believe those three are the sacred marriage from which all other gods descended," Sibja added. "Jinja, the wife with her two husbands, although I find it interesting that heretics cannot agree on whether Gavd or Retav is the da-husband."

"Which most call proof that all heretics are fools who try to make the gods so like Kowri that they would have marriages as we do." Alb didn't hide her disgust. "When there is no proof for which of two options is correct, one should reevaluate whether one has overlooked a third alternative or whether one might be so lost as to no longer be able to form a rational question. It does not take a follower of Lady Onidba to have that much logic at one's disposal."

"I assume Lady Divashi is not as popular," Dante guessed. The man did possess keen insight.

"The Lady of poisons is unpopular although she has followers, unlike Poque. I believe Regi a'Divashi was the last Kowri to leave sacrifices for that grand lady who once led the Kowri Empire to expand across space." Alb gave Regi a look that was too full of devilry and condescension. It was as if Regi's mother had taught Alb that exact expression. "When Kowri were first reaching for the stars, she was more beloved than Gavd. Young people flocked to leave offerings for her frim in the hopes that she would choose them for some grand adventure."

"For young people, the grand adventure is more important than the god," Dante muttered. Sibja drew in a quick breath and her ears tilted backwards. Dante's head jerked up. "No offense, ma'am. I suppose I'm speaking more for my people than yours, since I don't know yours well. But I do know that throughout history, there been any number of times that young people have flocked towards some adventure whether it be a new world or a new war, and some of them invoked God's name, less for God than to justify what they wanted."

Alb chuckled. "Sibja a'Iloxot, you don't need to feign dismay for a class full of first-year temple acolytes. You and I both know he's right."

Sibja huffed without saying anything to either agree with or contradict Alb. Regi reminded himself that he was an exalted with equal authority to these two ladies, but when an exalted of the Lady of punishment appeared that distressed, Regi did devoutly wish for a task in another room.

"Young people are the same everywhere," Alb said, humor now coloring her condescension. "Has Regi a'Divashi explained how he pledged himself to Poque and abandoned the temple?" Regi's fur bristled, but he couldn't defend himself from the truth. He had done that, and with the wisdom of hindsight, he knew he had been arrogant and angry and seeking to find a way to escape not just his home or his planet but his entire people. He had not been reasonable. However, once he had made his choice, he had never denied his Lady of wandering until a more deadly Lady had taken an interest in him.

"He has. I've known quite a few people who've done worse to get on one of the rockets to Mars."

"Mars? That does not translate."

"Our second planet. It's only been about thirty years since my people first set up a rudimentary settlement on Mars, so moving there is an adventure. Most young people dream of leaving Earth and braving the dangers of space to claim a spot on that world. Security is exceptionally tight, and despite that, there have been a few creative individuals who have found a way to steal someone's identity or stowaway among the livestock headed for Mars. Once they reach the settlement, it costs too much to send them back to Earth, and so they get their adventure."

Alb clapped her hands delightedly. "I would love to record those stories. Very few still read the oldest of Oba's sacred texts, but they include similar escapades. Young Kowri counted it as a grand triumph to greet a new world when they had been denied the blessings of parents and temple. They say the gods favored those who took such risks, or certain gods did anyway." Alb's eyes again lost focus. Regi wondered whether failing eyesight or a love of old stories caused that sense that she sometimes drifted away.

"It is more likely the gods noticed those who did so. One cannot be exalted without first being noticed, although god-touched and god-chosen are two distinctly different paths," Sibja said. She leaned back, her body language relaxing minutely. Regi's shoulders loosened at a sign of success so small that it might exist only in his imagination. However, he believed they were on the best path. Alb had begun to see similarities between the early Kowri explorers and huumans, and her word would go far to convince the scores of Kowri who remained silent on the matter of the Coalition crew and ship.

"Sitting in a room with others chosen by the gods, I can say it is the more difficult path," Alb said. "I am fortunate for reaching my age; the god's luck often outstrips our resources as exalteds before age can take us. But my Lady is the mildest of all the cold weather gods. I would say she chose the wrong season, but storytelling is a task for when the snow runs deep. What is the value of telling a story if everyone has too many tasks to sit and listen?"

"The librarian back home used to say that if someone wrote a story that no one ever read, it couldn't be rightly called a story," Dante agreed.

Alb propped her chin up with a delicate fist. Age had carved away the fat, leaving her as insubstantial as a tatbo tree swaying in the wind. "Do you believe your people possess followers of Oba or Divashi?" The question caught Regi off guard, and his gaze flew to Dante. The wrong answer could cross the boundary of impious and land in heretical territory.

"I am not up to the task of debating theology. If we can ever find my planet, there will be hundreds if not thousands of people who will happily debate the relationships between your gods and mine, but I have always made a point of avoiding any discussion of someone else's gods."

Alb smiled. "That is a rare bit of good sense coming from someone so young." She glanced in Regi's direction, and he was at a loss to interpret her gesture. She might be complimenting him on finding a reasonable outsider or implying that he lacked similar good sense.

As a young man, Regi had found temple exalteds confusing and distressing. In more recent years, he had convinced himself that he had felt small in their presence only because he had been young. And that conclusion was utterly wrong because her studied gaze made Regi want to apologize for all his sins. Being an adult had not cured that.

"I'll be honest, I'm not sure what you or Regi expect I can do to help any of this," Dante said with more volume than necessary in a small space.

Alb transferred her gaze to Dante, but her expression softened. "I expect you can help simply by proving that outsiders are capable of conversation that does not serve to insult the gods."

"The gods cannot hear their insults to take offense to them," Sibja said. She crossed her ankles and rotated one foot slowly, her gaze focused on that restless limb. "Iloxot is unbothered by insults, regardless of the source. I have listened to fathers condemn my Lady's name after I passed judgement and I have seen women fall to the ground and beg her for a mercy that neither she nor I would grant because punishment had been earned, and I know that my Lady is disturbed by neither. However, Kowri are as quick to take offense as any sapient creature."

"I always figured the good Lord was too great to get offended by any words I might say, although that did not prevent my grandmother from taking offense to those words," Dante said with a smile.

Alb studied Dante. "I wonder if you are god-touched."

Sibja snapped her head around to pin the woman with a horrified look.

Alb waved her hand as though dismissing Sibja as she might a stray flitt. "We are not in public, and I know you have entertained the same thought. The boy handles dops. In any other circumstances, we would have tossed him into the temple to see if the sacred animals claimed him."

Sitting bolt upright, Sibja appeared ready to fly into battle. "You cannot mean to take such a course of action."

"Of course not. Allowing an outsider into the temple proper would be sacrilegious, but it would make a good story." Her voice grew faint. "As a follower of the Lady Oba, I am allowed to seek good stories."

"I would appreciate it if this meeting were limited to topics more relevant to reality." Sibja's voice had a formality that made the hair of Regi's arms ripple with distress. Alb may have lost them critical support, and her eyes still had a distant, haunted emptiness that Regi feared might imply a feebleness of mind he had not noticed before.

After a second, Alb shook her head and pricked her ears so far forward that Regi could see the pink interior. "It would be a boon if we could get others to recognize that Dante is a reasonable being. Is there any excuse we could use for introducing Dante to a small society outside the temple?"

Dante glanced to Regi with such hope that Regi swallowed all his protestations about the danger. In the city, Dante might cause a mob, and when people could hide their hand in a sea of arms, they would allow themselves to commit evils that would not survive the light of even a cloudy day. Regi would not put Dante in that sort of danger, and he did not believe it would improve their situation anyway. They needed Kowri to speak to Dante, not whisper about him. "He has wished to ride pebafri. That would allow him to speak with the stable master and those who toil in the stables." And it would minimize the number of Kowri who had access to him.

Sibja laughed. "I had thought you reasonable, Dante a'Texas. Only children desperate to impress Gavd go near those great creatures."

"No offense, ma'am, but I grew up riding a similar beast called a horse. I'm more comfortable getting around on a horse's four feet than I am walking on my two."

"Given the punishment he suffered in captivity, it would seem appropriate to allow him some leeway in exploring." Alb emphasized the word punishment, and Sibja narrowed her eyes. If one counted slavery as a penance, that meant addressing any unfairness in the meting out of that suffering fell under the Lady Iloxot.

"Every exalted in the temple will know exactly what we're doing," she said.

"And yet, there is not an exalted in the temple who can stop you from doing it. You are the exalted of the Lady Iloxot and Jig will not contradict you."

"Jig?" Dante's voice danced as though he was amused by the name. Regi wished he had some godly insight into Dante's thoughts, but huumans appeared to differ from much of the universe, and the other huuman slaves had either died at the hands of the slavers or found ways to kill themselves to avoid the torment of slavery. Only Dante had persisted. Perhaps the Lady Divashi had given him the strength to endure whatever had driven the other huuman slaves to their death. That was an impious thought he would never speak aloud, but Dante was the one caring for the dops, and the Lady did love her animals.

"Jig a'Iloxot," Sibja said. "He believes your crew are victims of circumstances. He argues we should remove you from the ship, repair it with all haste and then toss the outsiders back across the border so they can return to their people. He is quite vociferous in his preferences, but we do not contradict each other, and he holds no animosity for any outsider."

"Dante would have to learn the specifics of riding the pebafri, and that would allow him to speak to those in the stable." Regi had taken lessons back when he had been one of those children hoping to impress Gavd. Stable masters were exacting in their care for the animals and would not allow anyone to ride until they had ensured that the rider could handle the pebafri without anyone dying, especially the pebafri. They worried more about animals being ridden over poor ground or allowed to eat noxious weeds than a rider breaking his neck.

Alb nodded slowly. "You would want to choose one of the stables on the outer edge of town. Those more closely associated with the spaceport would be aligned with Bekdi a'Gavd, and he questions the right of outsiders to breath his sacred air."

That was an understatement. "The temple has provided a fari, so I can seek out an appropriate stable."

"'Fari'?" Dante asked. Sometimes the translation matrix was inadequate, and Regi feared that it could fail at a critical time, but ironically it had, so far, handled discussion of gods with more facility than household items.

"A communication device that allows us to speak with those at a distance, like the communication relays on the pirate vessel allowed us to contact the Gavd ship."

"Oh, a phone. Got it," Dante said. "I guess the other slaves and I never talked about phones when we were on the ship, so this matrix didn't catch it." Dante tapped the side of his head.

"But you discussed gods?" Regi asked.

Dante blew out a breath, a gesture Regi could not understand despite the similarity to Dante's displays of humor. "We talked about gods, cursed gods, debated gods. At one point, Richard, Sophie and I put God on trial and decided he was a real bastard for letting us get taken by those pirates."

"'Bastard'?" Sibja asked.

"Huumans insult each other using bodily functions and references to marital status," Regi explained. He didn't understand the purpose of such insults because he would rather make factual statements about a person's lack of intelligence or tact, but Ter had a similar preference for metaphorical insults.

"That we do," Dante agreed. "And if I get to ride an alien horse and convince people I'm not a complete barbarian, that would be a win. I would also like to avoid being killed by self-righteous bigots who think I'm not worth a tinker's damn."

Regi would have asked for help translating part of that, but Alb spoke first. "I would greatly like to avoid your death because you, Dante a'Texas, are an interesting person. And I am old enough to say without qualification that there are too few interesting people in this universe. Your death would be a tragedy."

"That would be my opinion on the matter," Dante said with a two-finger touch to his forehead.

Sibja startled and looked to Regi, and only then did Regi consider that others might consider the gesture a mockery of the god tribute. However, the gesture was Dante's and Regi would not strip him of any part of himself he had maintained during his time in captivity.

Age had given Alb longer fur than a young Kowri might possess, and her smile grew so wide that the fur bunched at the corners of her eyes so she appeared to bristle like a dop. "Arrange for that, Regi a'Divashi. Let others see Dante for who he is, and perhaps we can change some Kowri minds."

Chapter Six

The Kowri didn't seem to have any concept of suburbs. There was only a dense village with four- and five-story buildings that ended at the edge of an equally dense wood. If anyone ever started a forest fire, Dante figured the town and shipyard would go up damn fast. But knowing Regi's people, they had some god of forest fires they relied on to prevent that from happening.

The universe was a damn strange place.

Once they left the wide, empty space around the space port, Regi had chosen a path that followed the edge of the town, so tall trees shaded the lane on one side, and the backs of potential apartment buildings lined the other. For one second, Dante considered making a joke about how alien worlds all looked a little like rural Canada, but he didn't figure Regi watched much B-level science fiction.

A few Kowri faces watched from upper windows, but so far everyone had kept their distance. Dante still felt alien gazes on his skin as he tried to ignore his own discomfort. Still, the way some leaned against open windowsills made him think about snipers. He wasn't sure how Kowri would handle an alien diving behind a tree, but he suspected they would not appreciate his assumption that a Kowri would shoot him in the back.

And he didn't even know if Kowri engaged in that sort of violence. They seemed like a knife-in-the-front kind of species. Even when Dante had gone to the temple during that first day on the planet, angry Kowri had tried to get in front of him to confront him. No one jumped him from the back. More than anything, that choice set them apart from the pirates. However, he suspected both groups were dangerous.

Like most of the Kowri, Regi was solidly made. His gray and black stripes reminded Dante of a monochrome tiger painted in velvet fur, which should be a warning that his people were hunters and designed to lurk in shadowed woods. Dante found those markings comforting on Regi. After all, Dante had always felt more at ease around animals than people.

"This place is amazing," Dante said. He needed to distract himself from the fear that had begun to make a return. He had thought the slavers had burned that out of him, but apparently not.

"I find most planets are remarkably similar. Life has certain requirements that even the gods cannot circumvent. However, I have missed worlds with large expanses of protected wilderness." Regi didn't hesitate in his easy stroll. Either he was not worried about an ambush, or he hid his emotions far better than Dante.

Dante angled his head upward. "That is not like any other planet." He studied the white and orange arches glowing against the blue sky. Fluffy clouds drifted past, obscuring parts, so they were above the atmosphere. Dante assumed they were planetary rings, but he had never seen a view from underneath.

Regi glanced up. "The planet where I grew up had rings. We lived so close to the center line that the rings appeared as a bright line that rose nearly straight up into the heavens."

Center line. Equator. The translator did have some glitches.

Regi cocked one ear toward Dante. "I assume your planets do not have rings, but surely you knew that such planets existed."

"Sure, I knew they could. Either Jupiter or Saturn has big rings, I can't remember which, and I've seen pictures from space." Dante turned to Regi. "But this... this is beautiful." Dante needed more descriptive words. The arches glowed, no doubt reflecting the sun, and it cast an almost magical glow on the town, including the blue-hued temple where Alb had her office. It gave the edges an orange tint. Dante had assumed it was a lopped-off pyramid, but as they walked around the side, he realized that the building was elongated.

"That temple is huge."

"The cold-season temple must house the most dangerous and most territorial animals, so it is larger than either the growing-season or harvest-season temples."

"So, those are the safe temples?" Dante wondered if they could visit those next time because the atmosphere around Regi's temple had been less than friendly. He'd liked Alb and Sibja, but when they'd passed the entrance, Dante had thought some Kowri had attempted to murder him by glaring.

"Iloxot, Lady of punishment, is a harvest-season god."

"So, not safe, but safer," Dante guessed. "And that makes sense since punishment is the harvest you get from your sins." Dante hadn't felt any sympathy for the bastard who'd killed his mother. He had harvested that sentence, and even if Dante had been against the death penalty before the trial, he couldn't regret the jury's decision. However, that was a detail Dante planned to keep to himself. He wasn't sure how aliens saw capital punishment, and he didn't want to either paint himself as a barbarian or give them ideas.

"The three-season temples are magnitudes larger."

"Larger?" Dante stumbled. He couldn't wrap his mind around a building that was magnitudes larger than something three or four times the size of Egypt's pyramids.

"Just as Retav ships are magnitudes larger than Gavd ships." Regi offered that detail in an almost bored tone.

Dante blinked, his brain going offline as he considered what that would mean. The Gavd ships surrounding the pirate vessel were enormous, and the pirate ship would dwarf human rockets. Earth had lost the technology race.

"The stables should be nearby. Hopefully they have deactivated the security. The outlying stables suffer from the insatiable curiosity of children, so they secure the fence line."

At one point, Dante had been one of those curious kids, begging to trade riding lessons for time mucking out stables. His parents had the money to pay for lessons, but his father had vetoed it unless Dante wanted to work with one of the English riding stables in town. He thought they looked smart in their suits as they went around the damn jumping course. Dante preferred shoveling horse shit. "I don't see much technology." Even the doorbell at Alb's house had been the sort that could be found on old schoolhouses: it swung, and a clapper slapped against the dome.

"Kowri prefer to hide our technology so it doesn't interfere with the forests."

"Another god?" Dante guessed.

A small smile graced Regi's face. "Lord Qis is the god of both old forests and secrets."

"A good god to avoid angering."

Regi touched his thumbs to his temples. "Most developed species eschew nature." Regi stopped and put a hand on the nearest tree—a huge specimen with a trunk so thick Dante wouldn't be able to reach around it.

Dante leaned against another tree, the rough bark familiar. "Plenty of humans do as well, but I like this, and most of my people would as well." Even city slickers liked tree-lined walks and quaint villages, although most drew the line at the inevitable remains of nature. Let them see one crusted over pile of dog poop or a half-eaten crow and they shrieked and covered their children's eyes. Dante had a vivid memory of a pack of reporters horrified at the horse poop littering a trail near the ranch. Range horses ate grass… which meant they pooped grass. After a day or two, the manure disintegrated, but the reporters picked their way around it and whispered loudly about trail management. So Dante understood Regi's frustration with his shipmates' prejudices.

Regi fingered a broad leaf. "Humans are unusual then." He drew out the "u" in humans so far that he turned the drawl into a new art form.

"Why? Because we're similar to yours?"

"Yes." After a moment of silence, Regi strode off. Even with his long legs, Dante had to break into a trot to catch up.

The fence was made of something like long rods of rebar, and a far gate with alien script on a sign had a silhouette of an animal that resembled a cross between a unicorn and an emaciated rhinoceros. Regi touched the gate, pulling his hand back quickly. Then his ears pricked forward, and he pushed the gate open. That was the reaction of someone who worried about an electric fence.

"This way," Regi said. He strode toward a building painted obnoxious green with icy blue trim. The gables of the building were open and giant fans turned slowly, moving air through even though the day was still. Regi opened a narrow door in the end of the stable and entered the dim building.

Dante had learned to judge people by their stables. A person who kept a stable with spotless concrete floors and the faint whiff of bleach cared more about appearances than the comfort of animals. One that stank and had deep straw clumped with waste had perfected laziness. This stable had the hallmarks of someone who cared for the animals. The warm smell of hay filled the air, and the animals had enough bedding that the few in their stalls had kicked some out. However, he would never mistake these creatures for horses.

The animals had huge heads, and they were as tall as Percherons although not as wide. Their faces were some bizarre combination of rhinoceros and horse and unicorn, but with none of the beauty of any of those animals. It had huge eyes and a bare head with only a short Mohawk of mane on the neck. A wide, blunt horn in the middle of their skull looked ready to ram an enemy, and a pair of shorter and sharper ones flanked large nostrils.

"Welcome, exalted." A large Kowri came out from behind a rolling rack of feed. He propped his pitchfork against a round bale of what must pass for local hay.

"Greetings." Regi touched his temples, and the new Kowri did the same. "I had hoped to show my friend the pebafri."

"Ah, well you can see I have some of the best on the planet. I had a beautiful girl with white legs, but she wandered off toward the temple, and you know how it goes. The gods choose, and we are left with what remains." His ears swiveled before going back to what Dante thought of as a resting position.

Regi changed the subject, so maybe complaining about the gods was rude. "Dante rode an animal similar to our pebafri on his home planet before pirates removed him from his world to care for the dops they had stolen from Kowri worlds."

The stable hand's eyes widened, although Dante wasn't sure exactly what part of the statement had surprised him. Kowri seemed as reluctant to get near dops as the pirates had been, but Regi acted surprised every time Earth had some similarity to Kowri worlds, so that could cause the reaction.

"I heard you had animals that you rode the way we ride horses, and I had to ride one."

The new Kowri laughed. "Spoken like a true rider. I had not thought outsiders rode animals."

This was the plan—Dante had to impress these xenophobic aliens. He had to bury his own urge to hide his feelings behind a facade and let others see him as a person. "My people still debate whether anyone exists in the universe outside our own people, so I am too new to the universe to know what outsiders are likely to do. I only know that many of my people enjoy horse riding. Are your pebafri safe to handle?" Dante nodded toward the closest animal. Now that the shock had passed, he could see the stark beauty in the strong line of their muscle and the curve of their horns.

"No animal that large is safe; Gavd chose a favorite who is more than capable of defending himself," he said. "But one with a strong will can handle them." He studied Dante, not hiding his doubt that Dante was up to the task. However, riding was the only part of this plan that Dante was confident about. He'd gentled wild horses and trained rescue horses to ride trails. He knew animals. He knew very little besides animals.

"Can we hire a pebafri and hire your time as Dante attempts to reconcile his knowledge of horses and our pebafri?" Regi asked.

The stable hand wiped his palms on his pants—a gesture Dante had seen thousands of times in the stables. "I would not ask payment from an exalted. I am Siger. I own the stable, and when you called, it was I who spoke with you, Regi a'Divashi."

"The twin blessings and thank you for inviting us into your stable." Regi made that strange thumb touch gesture in front of his chest.

"Thank you," Dante echoed. He didn't want to offend anyone by wishing blessings on them, especially since Regi's people considered bad luck the first blessing. Dante had been raised to avoid wishing bad luck on others. "I haven't ridden any creature that large, so I hope you can give me some instruction."

Siger hooked his thumbs into his waistband. "Those who have not ridden pebafri usually insist they know enough to ride one."

"Or that Gavd will guide their hand," Regi said softly. Regi wrinkled his nose. "I was a precocious child who overestimated how much the gods watched over me."

"Most young people do," Siger said. "I once cried after eating sweets because I was sure my mother's god would tell her that I had broken her rules. I had not yet learned that the gods see little of what we do."

"Their gaze is too large for this world," Regi agreed. "However, I hope the Lady Divashi will continue to guide us as long as any dops or slaves are held by pirates who hide along our border."

Siger's ears dipped backward, which probably meant that he didn't think Regi wise for relying on his goddess. Dante understood the concern. Any goddess named after poison seemed like a questionable choice as a patron, but it seemed like Divashi hadn't given either of them much of a choice.

Dante suspected the good Lady had seen him, making him either god-touched or god-chosen in the Kowri culture. After all, he'd dropped his cleaning water, which had stalled him in the room as he worked to clean his mess before any pirates caught him. And then the door had jammed, causing the locking mechanism to engage. Dante had been stuck in that room when he heard unfamiliar shouts and pounding feet. When Regi had triggered the exterior latch, Dante had tripped over him and nearly brained himself on the far wall before Regi's second in command had pinned him to the floor. In Regi's terms, that would be an excess of the goddess's first blessing. Dante hoped Divashi had lost track of him now that he was surrounded by so many Kowri.

Dante decided to change the subject to something he could discuss without offending anyone. "On my world, I cared for horses and took those with no experience out on rides. I know the danger of underestimating animals. Since I have never ridden a pebafri, I know I need the guidance of one with enough experience to keep me from making a mistake." He offered his best Texas smile.

"You have passed your temple years," Siger said with a huff.

Dante frowned at Regi.

"You've finished your temple education. You aren't a child who doesn't know how the world works," Regi explained.

"My father would disagree," Dante said before his normal reticence could veto his mouth.

"Fathers," Siger said in a weary tone. Apparently, some experiences were universal. "A pebafri is a dangerous animal for one whose experienced is limited, and even with instruction and guidance, your safety is not guaranteed. I would not wish for you to underestimate the danger in falling off an animal or getting thrown off if your behavior annoys the beast."

Dante looked at the pebafri's massive legs. He doubted it could buck fast enough or high enough to get him off, and Dante hadn't fallen off a horse in years. He'd had a couple of horses take spills and he'd gone down with them, so riding had its dangers. "I will take that risk. I have been locked inside a ship for long enough that bruises or broken bones would be a small price to pay. However, I promise to listen to every instruction so I can minimize the risk."

"Any rider who has been on an animal more times than they have fingers has experienced an intimate relationship with the ground. Pebafri have no patience for mistakes."

So they were like riding a stallion or a mare going into heat. Dante had been fool enough to do that a few times. It wasn't as if the stable could allow horses to go without exercise because they were hormonal on a particular day. "I will keep that in mind," Dante promised.

"Follow. I will show you the equipment we use to tame these animals and give you a brief description of the guidance and control."

"I hope that's a fancy way of saying reins."

"That word did not translate. What are reins?" Siger moved toward the back of the stable. Dante followed close at his heels, and Regi trailed behind.

"A way to control horses," Dante offered.

"Then I will show you reins."

"Dante." Regi put a hand on Dante's arm, and a shiver went up his spine. "The wilderness is dense, and you do not have a phone. Do not leave the road or lose sight of the town unless you have someone with you who can call for help if a situation arises that you need assistance."

That was a reasonable concern. "I promise," Dante said.

Regi huffed. "And try to avoid breaking any critical or necessary bones."

Dante had to school his features to avoid laughing. He hadn't expected that sort of admonition. "I will do my best to keep any bone-breaking to small ones."

Regi wrinkled his nose, and the hair along his nostrils fluffed up. The expression was unbearably cute.

"I'll be fine," Dante said. And he would have a chance to hang around the stable and talk to the Kowri who came to ride. Alb was right that they had to change the perception of the average Kowri, and riders bonded over a shared love of their animals.

Besides, after months trapped in a tin can, he longed to be in the open. Maybe pebafri weren't horses, but it was possible Dante would never again see any horse, much less Marengo. Marengo and Blue had left a hole in his heart, but Dante had to move on. This was his life now. Peaches and some big, horned bastards were what he had left, and he had to find a way to make his peace with that. It was all he could do.

Chapter Seven

Regi poked his computer with more vehemence with every passing second. While Siger was a more appropriate guide than Regi who had not sat atop a pebafri in fifteen years, he still felt an itch to rush to Dante's side and provide some empty assurance that all would be fine. Dante was a grown man who needed neither the reassurance nor Regi's presence, but still... the feeling persisted. It left Regi in an intemperate mood, and his computer was suffering the consequences.

Two crew had gotten in an altercation over a perception that one had neglected his duties, leaving the other to do the work. These petty complaints would only increase the longer they were all confined on the ship. The crew feared the Kowri Empire—with good cause—and that stress would seek a convenient outlet. Regi would normally speak with them in confinement, but his own mood was too unpredictable to deal with angry crew. He routed the report to Vk and left it in her capable hands.

Regi had moved on to the more mundane reports required of a security head when his door chime announced the arrival of Captain Cota. With a sigh, Regi thumbed the door controls.

Cota stood with his thumbs hooked to his utility belt. "I have a meeting with a council of exalteds," he announced without preamble.

"Captain." Regi stopped, too horrified to form words properly.

He took a step into the room and the door closed behind him. "I hoped you could provide insight into the political structure of the temple before I'm due to speak with them."

Regi blinked, his horror precluding any thought of reasonable discussion. After a moment, he reined in his emotions. "My insight would include avoiding the exalteds until the ship is repaired and we are on the far side of the border."

Cota's neck muscles corded and relaxed in a blink. "You fear violence."

"I expect violence if the wrong individuals are aggravated," Regi corrected him.

"Then perhaps you can identify those individuals so I can avoid violence."

Again, words escaped Regi like fish darting into the shadows formed by the roots of a grand tree when a predator appeared at the side of their pool. "I do not know these exalteds well enough to offer such advice," he said. "I can only advise you to avoid any prolonged conversations." Regi was aware that the captain had been attempting to speak with Kowri who walked too near the ship, but he had not known that any exalted had paid attention to his requests.

His mouth curled into a wry smile. "I suspect that is no longer an option. I assume refusing to meet with them would cause significant consternation."

It would, and from the expression on Cota's face, he knew as much. Regi wished he had spent more time mitigating Cota's curiosity and political machinations, but he had been distracted by temple issues: the matter of Divashi's intentions and discussions of political options with Alb. "I am unsure what you hope to gain."

Cota settled into a seat. "I am aware that you would keep me on the ship and away from other Kowri."

Resentment washed through Regi. "Because as a Kowri, I am arrogant and disrespect the autonomy of others." Regi had heard as much from any number of Coalition members. They painted Regi with the same broad brush they used on his entire species, ignoring the sins committed by the Coalition in generations past.

Cota huffed. "Because you are obsessive in ensuring the safety of the crew. I will admit that I questioned my superiors' motives in assigning a Kowri to lead the security team, especially given that we patrol the border with the Empire. However, I quickly grew to respect their decision because you prioritize the crew. I have served on this ship with Ter for many years, and every security officer before you enforced the rules without taking care to protect Ter from the consequences of his own poor relationships with others, but his subordinates last longer now because you blunt the worst of his temper. You minimize the consequences of any complaints Ter might file while allowing him to vent his spleen on you." Cota leaned forward. "I trust you with our security."

Regi stared at the captain, not sure how to respond. He had assumed Cota had not noticed that certain complaints brought up at the officers' review meetings were never filed with the official reports. And had he realized that Cota was aware, he would have expected a complaint from the captain. "Then you know I hope to protect you from the xenophobia of other Kowri."

"I do," Cota said. "I am not a tactically brilliant thinker, but I am good with managing personalities."

"Except Ter." The words slipped out before Regi could edit his thoughts. The day had provided more stress than he could process into a reasonable response.

"Including Ter," Cota said with some amusement. "I aggravate him to provide a target for his infamous temper. I appreciate that you manage the aggravation of his staff with more facility than previous security chiefs, and so you improve moral. However, Ter still requires an outlet."

"You're manipulating him." Regi's world view slid to the side as all previous interactions took on new meaning.

"Of course I am. The man has a mind that can advance technology that most sapient creatures can barely comprehend; however, he would inspire his staff to commit murder if someone didn't intervene." Cota huffed his amusement, although Regi found nothing humorous in the image of Ter's staff revolting against his unreasonable temper. They had come close a few times, but with this new insight, Regi could see that Cota had drawn Ter's ire by enforcing some little-used rule or creating a training game that caused Ter to curse in so many languages and with such creativity that the translation matrix failed, making Regi's scalp itch as the tingle grew too great.

"I didn't think you noticed," Regi said.

"So, you believed I was a great fool."

"Only a minor one. I don't believe it falls under the captain's duties to protect apprentice-level technicians from the engineer's wrath."

"It's the captain's duty to provide for the crew. That's why I must speak with the Kowri exalteds."

Regi considered the statement in light of his new understanding of the captain. "That is dangerous," he reiterated. Even an individual with such insight into the needs of others could not blunt the anger Kowri carried for the Coalition that had disrespected and stolen from them.

"Are you refusing to brief me?" Cota asked, his voice gentle. Despite the tone, a shiver made Regi's fur ripple.

"I am not. I would never withhold information from you, captain."

"Would you not? Not even to protect me? Protect the crew?"

Regi opened his mouth but remained silent. He could not deny the charge without lying. Perhaps he might have obfuscated, but he was unexpectedly uncertain about the captain. The man was shrewder than Regi expected, and that left him unsure about how to handle him. "The safest course is to repair the ship as quickly as possible and leave Kowri space."

"Without you?" Cota asked.

"Would you prefer I remain?" Shock made Regi's voice louder than he had intended.

"No. I would prefer you continue as my security officer. However, the Kowri seem to believe the proper place for an exalted is the temple—at least I assume as much from the number of times they have requested your presence."

Regi cringed.

"I understand the mistakes made in the past, but I need your insight before I speak with these temple exalteds. Do these individuals resemble an Efhtee assembly or a Rit'let'telaic legislature or a Vajroon court? Is their decision-making authority more closely related to the Coalition Officer Councils or the Regent Convocation? I know the exalteds vote, but does each individual's voice speak as loudly as any other?"

Regi wished he had answers. Perhaps Cota would be more capable of using the information than Regi had given him credit for. "I do not know any of these exalteds. In every group, some carry more authority because of age or an ability to form informal alliances, but I cannot lay out political realities that I struggle to understand myself. Alb and Sibja have spoken with me and a few Kowri including Bekdi a'Gavd and Leevshi a'Dicia are united in their hatred of outsiders. They want us gone, but they feel that since Divashi revealed this ship, the ship belongs to the Empire."

Cota blanched. Perhaps now he understood the dire situation they faced. "Do others agree with this perspective?"

"Most are silent, unsure about where to lead the Empire when a god has done something no god has ever done before."

"I thought you followed a goddess?"

Regi smoothed down his arm hair. His emotional state was such that he could not relax enough to lay the hairs down flat. "Your language is binary—male and female. My language has three sexes, but our pronouns are ungendered. I do follow a goddess, but when I speak of the more universal distress of a god perceiving events outside the

Empire, your translation matrix creates a distinction where none exists in Kowri language."

Cota tangled his fingers into a complex knot. "Ean would remove a small bone from her own body with a spoon if you would share even that much linguistic insight with her."

"No doubt," Regi agreed. She had, early in his assignment, peppered him with questions about Kowri language and psychology—none of which he had answered. She was likely dying one hair at a time to be this close to her answers and be confined to the ship. "If one were to consider only the exalteds and no others, the government would resemble the true democracy of the Filixi. The rest of the Kowri trust the exalteds to lead. Complaints from citizens are taken to a temple, and if a resolution is not found, the debate moves to the three-season temple. However, Kowri have no frame of reference for diplomacy. Not only am I completely ignorant about how they might respond, but I fear the exalteds themselves are unaware of the ways they might react. Fear is dangerous. Fear and ignorance are worse."

"It is a dire situation," Cota said, "and I plan to apologize for the entire Coalition. Every captain assigned to the border knows that to be the primary responsibility of any officer who can get the Kowri to listen."

"Abject apologies might sooth certain ruffled feathers; however, if you get some Kowri to acknowledge your perspective, that could push other Kowri to oppose you if only to maintain the balance and ensure that those more favorable to outsiders do not gain ascendancy. And you cannot imply that our gods exist only in our imaginations. It is factually incorrect, and we have the technology to prove as much." Regi would have continued to lay out the political dangers, only his communicator gave a sharp tone.

"Yes?" Regi answered.

Vk said in a strained voice, "I believe you should open your door."

Regi traded concerned looks with Cota. "Why?"

"Because I would avoid someone dying of poison," Vk responded. It was an enigmatic response for a practical woman. Regi triggered the mechanism and the dop Dante had named Peaches waddled in, one of her smaller male attendants following.

"Should those be loose in the corridor?" Cota pulled his feet up, propping his shoes on the edge of Regi's desk to keep them away from quills.

"She has never shown an interest in leaving her room in the past." Regi walked around the desk, surprised when she tried to climb his pant leg. She was larger than most, and the effort entailed panting and grunts that sounded distinctly unhealthful. Regi offered the flat of his hand, and she trundled onto it. The male tried to follow, and she chittered a warning at him, leaving him to cry in the corner of the office. She had disallowed any courtships at this time.

"Regi?" Vk leaned around the corner, sticking only her head in the office.

"I shall take her outside. Perhaps she has decided to attend the temple or return to the woods," Regi said. Peaches rattled her quills with anger and hissed. The sound made Cota flinch.

"That does not sound safe," Vk observed.

"It is not, but Dante would have more familiarity with her noises than I do." Just because Regi was an exalted of Divashi did not mean he could read her creatures the way some could. His mother had been able to watch the way her dafs croana curled into a knot and could predict the outcome of a pregnancy from it, but he lacked any commensurate skill with dops.

"Maybe you should call him," Cota suggested.

That was a wise suggestion. Dante had not been able to carry a phone since he had no legal identity in the communication system, but any stable hand who had escorted him during their ride would have one. Regi pulled out his own phone and requested communication with all staff of the stables owned by Siger a'Gavd.

An unfamiliar voice answered. "Twin blessings of the gods to you."

"I am seeking the outsider Dante a'Texas."

"The hairless one?" another voice asked.

"Yes," Regi said. "I require his assistance in regard to a dop that is fond of him." That would inspire someone to provide information. If his mother's dafs croana made others uncomfortable, a dop terrified them.

"I have not seen him," one voice said. One at a time, a half dozen others concurred. Regi did not hear the deeper tones of Siger. A sourness filled his stomach.

"Then I would speak with Siger a'Gavd," he said.

"He has left."

"I requested communication with all staff of the stables. Surely he is staff at his own stable, so why has he not answered?"

A long pause followed, and Regi began walking toward the exit, his mind spinning in a dozen ridiculous directions. "I have found his phone," a woman answered. "It was on the floor of one of the stalls, so it likely fell from his pocket. I will return it to him when he is back from his ride. You may call for him then."

"Are you sure he is riding?" Regi paused at the top of a ladder, cursing the angle that meant all lifts were offline. He could not hold the dop, the phone and the ladder at one time, but his instincts screamed at him that he needed to move.

"He took the pebafri he has been working to gentle," she said. "Siger will return when the sun is lower. May I tell him who seeks his attention?"

"Exalted Regi de Exalted Minait a'Otutha qee Pertin e Rel, favorite of Divashi, Lady of poisons, disorder, change and new beginnings," he said, using the formal titles he had hesitated to claim in the past. Something was wrong, and if he had to use his little temple clout to ensure Dante's safety, he would. A hiss on the other end revealed the staff's surprise. Without any additional pleasantries, Regi disconnected the phone and shoved it into a pocket before flinging himself down the ladder with one hand.

Something was wrong, and if Peaches was involved, it was a wrong large enough for the Lady Divashi to see and deem significant enough for her involvement.

Chapter Eight

Dante stretched his neck. He might have grown up on the back of a horse, but these pebafri had a much different gait. Instead of the rocking motion of a gaited horse or even the bone-shivering trot of his first horse—a cranky old gelding called Skip—the pebafri had a lurching motion, front to back. Part of his brain felt like he was on a horse, but every uncomfortable jerk reminded him that he was on an alien creature from another planet.

Dante breathed out and closed his eyes as he searched for that moment where the animal's movement became his. However, his beast did a quick two-step that made Dante's eyes fly open and his body tighten around his spine in preparation for the animal to start bucking. The pebafri turned to look at Dante before snorting.

Apparently, they were not destined to reach any accord. Sometimes a rider and an animal didn't mesh. Aggravation still circled in Dante's gut. He had pinned too many hopes on the idea of escaping the metal walls of the ship, and reality was not living up to the many daydreams he had tended over the previous months. He had asked Siger for an animal with some spirit, not a demon focused on scraping him off on the nearest tree.

Siger guided his huge black pebafri up a slope between two trees with limbs that drooped almost like a weeping willow. Something had eaten all the lower branches and foliage. Long strips of gray bark were missing, revealing pinkish sapwood underneath, and Dante guessed some alien version of deer. If Regi's people respected nature the way

Regi suggested, the presence of deer implied the presence of predators. That made Dante study the trees for any shadowed forms. "Do you have large predators in the area?" Dante asked.

"I do not see any at this time, but if I identify one, I shall point to it," Siger said. That wasn't exactly what Dante had asked, but he had grown used to the translator's near misses. Siger weaved through the forested area, following faint paths between dense bushes, and up a steep slope. Siger's long-legged beast leaned into the angle but maintained a placid nature that made Dante wonder if it was overfed. In contrast, when Dante's pebafri reached that point in the trail, he dug his front feet into the loose rock and rocketed forward.

When they reached the top, Dante settled back into the saddle and rolled his shoulders to release some of the tension. He had spent so long telling tenderfoots to relax when he took them on range rides that he felt like he shouldn't have to keep giving himself the same reminder. Dante's animal closed the distance and stretched out a neck, probably to take a bite out of Siger's pebafri. Dante pulled his creature's head around and earned another baleful glare.

"So what is this specific pebafri's name?" He had asked earlier and been offered only *"pebafri"*, which meant that he had phrased the question badly. Dante patted the pebafri's neck. He'd found adding a little kindness to a firm hand on the reins worked best.

"We call him Goddess's Brown."

"I thought pebafri belonged to a god, not a goddess." Dante had trouble keeping track of all the various gods, but he figured a little curiosity about the gods was a good way to convince Kowri that he wasn't an asshole. Maybe the Coalition had trouble dealing with believers, but Dante lived in Texas, a land famous for freedom, self-made men and women, and hard-core religion. Texans knew how to turn religion into a weapon of mass destruction against the federal government, so Dante never underestimated the lengths a person would go to in defense of their God. Or in the case of the Kowri, their gods.

"I'm not sure which goddess he was named to honor. I was a middling student of theology and there are many goddesses one might hope to please." Siger's voice had a terse quality that might imply that he disapproved of the topic or that he needed more fiber in his diet. Dante found it hard to tell. When Siger urged his pebafri between two trees and up a slope, Dante accidentally turned his in the opposite direction. Dante corrected his handling. A horse turned away from leg pressure, but pebafri leaned into it. Siger's instruction had been clear, but Dante was fighting a lifetime of habits.

His animal and Siger's were so different that Dante suspected one of them lacked either breeding or training. Siger's pebafri was languid and took every opportunity to grab a mouthful of grass. He was as lazy as any trail horse Dante had ever put a greenhorn on. While Dante would never call Goddess's Brown flighty because he showed no interest in running away from anything, but he did have a twitchiness that came close. He tended to jump toward stimulus instead of away from it. If Dante wasn't careful, he would take a chunk out of Siger's mount before this ride was over. Dante doubted that would improve his reputation.

"How do you judge quality in a pebafri?" Dante asked.

"If they run well." Siger kicked his animal and darted through the trees. This was a dangerous game to play with someone on a new animal, but Dante kicked his own pebafri and raced after him. Siger glanced over his shoulder and then turned his animal to the left.

"I don't think I'm comfortable enough in the saddle for barrel racing," Dante said, trying to make his words light with humor. He didn't know how much of that translated, but hopefully the tone came across. Dante didn't want to sound like a know-it-all who told the guy that he had no business encouraging a rider to take risks on an unfamiliar animal. That was how accidents happened, and Dante remembered that Regi carried an anelace to offer a quick end to pebafri who might break a leg. He didn't want an animal to suffer because Siger wanted to issue some challenge.

"I don't think an outsider will ever get comfortable in a pebafri's saddle," Siger countered. "That animal is sacred to Gavd."

"I respect that," Dante said. He focused on guiding his animal away from a thick tree trunk.

"Outsiders have no respect," Siger said.

Dante's head jerked up. Siger kicked his pebafri, sending him scrambling up the slope.

"Have I offended you in some way?" Dante called. Already Siger was half-hidden by the trees. He looked downslope, and the cold expression on his face made Dante's guts turn to ice. He'd seen that expression on homophobes in Texas and slavers on the alien ship. Disgust and disdain transcended species. Worse, the Kowri communication network used phones keyed to an individual, and Dante hadn't qualified to get one, so he couldn't call for help. Five minutes earlier, Dante had loved that Siger had taken him deep into the woods, but right now fear burned the base of his throat.

"You came to our sacred world."

"Your gods brought us," Dante countered. He was a good sixty percent sure that was the truth.

"Gavd didn't bring outsiders to this world. If any god did, it was Divashi, the poisoner, the destroyer of life. Gavd does not lead us to yield in the face of outsider impiety." Siger urged his pebafri faster. Dante urged his own animal up the steep slope. The nature of the Kowri world with civilization ending in a sharp line that left untouched wilderness meant that he wasn't as confident he could find his way back to the town. In Texas, he'd had his phone, the distant rumble of a truck on the highway over the rise, a line of power cables. Civilization always lurked right around the corner.

"Siger!" Dante called. Maybe this was a cruel form of hazing. The dislike wasn't faked, but Dante told himself that Siger wouldn't act on the feeling. He only wanted to vent his displeasure. Dante got it. The Kowri had their nice, isolated empire with an impervious boundary, and here came Regi and Dante and all sorts of outsiders threatening their sense of security. Dante suspected he understood that better than Regi did. Regi talked as if his people's xenophobia was illogical enough to defy explanation, which was naive.

Siger reached the crest of a wooded hill and whipped his pebafri around. Something in his gaze made Dante stop his animal. Without warning, Siger drove his animal straight downhill at Dante. Dante's animal screamed and threw his head into the air, rearing back, sharp hooves cutting through the air. The other pebafri bared his teeth and Siger kicked his heels into the animal's sides. All Dante could do was hold on as his animal screamed and charged uphill. Dante tightened his legs and kept his body low as he struggled to move with his animal. He abandoned any attempt to regain control in favor of not breaking his neck.

Siger brought his whip down on Dante's arm, and fire coursed through his body, but months as a slave had inured him to that sort of pain. It was familiar, and Dante leaned away from Siger, trusting that the stable master would not risk hitting his own animal. He trusted wrong. Siger's whip came down on the pebafri's neck, and Goddess's Brown shoulder-slammed the other pebafri, sending it stumbling downslope. Dante's leg had been caught between the animals, and now it ached. Even though it hurt less than the whip mark, Dante knew that sort of injury could cause much more damage. Crush injuries could kill hours later when the victim thought they had survived.

However, Dante had no time to worry about that now. Siger was downhill and galloping his pebafri as if he were on a racetrack. The problem was that the uneven ground and rock made an accident more likely than not. Dante held on as his animal careened down hills of loose shale. It slammed into one tree with his shoulder, and Dante felt the reverberation through his entire body. A horse would have broken a leg, but the pebafri screamed and jackknifed before breaking free of the trees and racing along a low ridge in pursuit of Siger and his pebafri. Dante held on for dear life through the most dangerous ride of his life.

The pebafri found its stride and Dante hoped he might survive. Then the animal lost his footing. He went off the edge of a shallow escarpment, and Dante felt the roll begin. He couldn't survive if the pebafri landed on him, so he kicked loose from the stirrups and threw himself backward into the gravel. The pebafri rolled, legs kicking in the air for a moment. He slid before he righted himself and bolted to his feet, legs sprawled and braced as though he expected the ground to betray him as well.

"Easy, boy," Dante crooned, hoping to get close enough to grab the reins. The pebafri took one look at him and bared his teeth before bolting away through the trees after Siger.

Well, fuck.

Chapter Nine

Perhaps it was an abuse of power, but Regi's anxiety over his inability to reach Siger on the communicator led him to request a hover, even before walking down the ramp to reach the ground. Few Kowri could navigate on a hover without endangering either themselves or the pedestrians with whom they shared the travelways. However, Regi had spent his childhood trying to master both the hover and the pebafri to improve his odds of serving Gavd. His success with the pebafri had been middling at best, but he had excelled with the hover, the favorite vehicle of Gavd's devotees when they hoped to move about town with any speed.

Unwilling to wait for the temple acolyte to appear with the vehicle, Regi trotted toward Siger's stable. He might have been tempted to break into a run, but the dop which Dante had named Peaches clung to his shirt close to Regi's cheek. The creature's constant chittering did nothing to soothe Regi's nerves. Whatever was going on, the lady Divashi's creature was as displeased as Regi.

Regi had left the port behind and was jogging a tree-lined lane when a temple acolyte appeared, darting between common folk as he clutched a hover in his arms. "Exalted! The temple said you sent an urgent request for a hover and that your communication device's location suggested that you were running. They ordered me to deliver this with all possible speed." The acolyte offered the hover.

Regi touched his temples. "Thank you for bringing it so quickly. I have some need to get to Siger's stable, and there is a chance that the situation with the outsider known as Dante a'Texas is..." Regi stopped, unsure what he should say.

He had no evidence that anything was wrong. While communication devices were intended to work across the globe, technology did fail. He remembered his mother's stories of when she had been an acolyte of Otutha and the communicator kept failing to include her any time a pregnant Kowri requested assistance in birth from the growing season temple. Everyone had dismissed it as a simple malfunction in the technology, and it had been. Of course, it had also been the bad luck that signaled that his mother was not an acolyte but an exalted.

All the other devotees of Lady Otutha had been called away to various tasks, but his mother had never attended those requests because the technology that was supposed to group Kowri into logical units to facilitate communication—units such as all midwives who worked in a certain town or all Kowri who work at Siger's stable—had failed. And so, when the exalted of Ectipic had gone into labor months before her time, only Regi's mother was available and Otutha had guided her hands to perform a near miracle to save the child.

However, such technology failures were common enough that in her story, every Kowri assumed the technology's failure had been mundane rather than divine. A technician had taken apart two different transmitters, and a coder had been searching through the command functions to understand how Minaita a'Otutha had become partially invisible to the communication network. Most technology failure was a failure of electrons and alloys, not a sign that the gods had intervened.

Which implied that Regi's inability to reach Dante and Siger was likely unimportant. But the huge old dop who sat on his shoulder still drove his fears. The acolyte watched, his ears forward and his eyes wide with concern.

"Please tell the exalted of Ectipic that there is a situation at Siger's stable and that his wisdom might well be required later." Regi trusted Nawr to handle such information without later using it to condemn Regi as hysterical when it turned out that Siger's communication device had a programming failure and had fallen off the net.

The acolyte's eyes grew wider. "Should I request Nawr a'Ectipic attend you at the stables?"

Regi wanted to agree with the tacit suggestion. He wished some exalted who had a better understanding of the world would take over all these problems and allow Regi to return to managing drunken crew and Cota's ridiculous drills. However, that would require denying his god, and Regi was not foolish enough to take such a step.

"Ask what direction his god leads," Regi said. He gestured at the dop on his shoulder. "Mine leads to the stable."

Not wanting to waste more time on discussion, Regi stepped onto the hover and, for a moment, struggled to find his balance. He leaned, and the hover careened left before Regi compensated. For one horrible second, he thought he might land in the dust with a bruised posterior, but he found his balance and his body remembered the tiny movements required to control the machine. Regi focused on a point far down the road and let himself lean slightly forward. The hover responded, and soon Regi was skimming down the walk at an unsafe speed.

Unwilling to give up on that distant point of focus, he dodged around pedestrians and animals using instinct more than forethought. On his shoulder, Peaches clung to his shirt with her tiny paws, her nails scratching at his neck. Her chittering had quieted. Dops were famous for their slow and methodical movements, and Peaches might have been imprisoned in the pirate ship her whole life, but despite the newness of this experience, she kept her quills tucked close, their poison contained. That was enough to convince him that he was on the right track. Peaches had calmed because the lady Divashi willed it so.

With the advantage of the hover's speed, Regi reached the stable in mere minutes. The corral had been empty this morning, but now a dozen saddled pebafri waited, stamping the ground until dust swirled about their legs and settled on their coat. A young woman with particularly brilliant white stripes finished tightening a bridle before she looked as Regi stepped off the hover.

"We can give no rides to acolytes of Gavd today," she said. She must've been harried to miss the dop who rode on his shoulder, and that made Regi's stomach sour even more.

"I am a follower of Divashi, not Gavd. And I come here seeking the outsider follower of Texas."

She whirled about and studied him with wide eyes. "Are you Regi a'Divashi?" The question was foolish given how few devotees of Divashi lived on any given world. Regi was the only one on this planet, so his possession of the dop should be enough to confirm his identity. However, Regi did not wish to in his excess of frustration alienate the woman.

"I am," he said. He expected her to offer some words, but she dashed into the stable. Regi's heart constricted until he had trouble drawing a full breath. He was trying to convince his trembling legs to carry him into the stable when Siger appeared at the door.

His gaze searched for Regi, and he brought his thumbs up to his temples when they made eye contact. "Exalted, I had meant to call you, but time is of such importance that I let the task fall to the wayside."

"What has happened?"

Siger winced. "An excess of bad luck."

Bad luck and opportunity, the twin blessings of the gods. Regi never should have sent Dante out without him, not when Regi was uncomfortably aware of how difficult the gods could make life when it came to their favorites. Even if no temple would ever recognize an outsider as an exalted, Regi knew that Dante had Divashi's favor.

"What happened?" he repeated. The words stuck in his throat so he could manage no more than that.

"I was leading Dante on a trail toward Thrice Mountain when I heard a cry behind me. When I turned, I saw that his pebafri had stepped badly and was sliding down an embankment."

"Dante?" Regi asked with alarm. Everyone who learned to ride the great pebafri had fallen at some point, so falling did not imply that he was dead or even injured. Parents often joked that the bones of young Kowri were made of rubber because of how often Kowri youth fell while being reckless. But Dante was no youth, nor was he a Kowri. He was a fragile species with bones that were far less dense and a throat structure where food and oxygen must navigate the same space through means of clever biological trapdoors. Bevti had warned that Dante was far too fragile to risk strenuous activities.

"Where is he?"

Siger winced and his ears dipped in a show of dismay and submission.

Regi took a step forward. "Where is he?" His brain summoned images of Dante broken and gasping, lying on a stable blanket that grew red with blood as they waited for healers to arrive. It was hard for him to breathe, and his chest burned with a scream that threatened to escape.

"I was riding Goddess's Brown, so when I attempted to follow him, I was unable to."

Dante's thoughts flickered as the information failed to integrate into the picture Regi had started to form. "'Follow him'? 'Unable'?"

With a grimace, Siger gestured toward a huge pebafri tethered to the stable fence. "Goddess's Brown is not well tamed to the saddle. When I attempted to follow the outsider, Goddess's Brown objected to the terrain and bolted. My staff tells me that you called for me, but I broke my phone when I fell from the saddle. And I had to chase Goddess's Brown for so long, that I was unwilling to risk the outsider's safety by searching for him alone. I required more assistance, so I returned to get help."

Peaches was growing more agitated, her tiny nails scratching Regi's neck and shoulder. Regi understood her concern. The stable hand had said Siger left his phone in the stable. "Why would you choose an animal not yet broken to the saddle when you were escorting one who has never before been on the great pebafri?"

Siger drew himself up. "Because he is named after your goddess. He is the Lady Divashi's Brown. I had thought it auspicious given that Dante a'Texas has a marked preference for the Lady's animals." Siger gestured towards the dop perched on Regi's shoulder. "I should have cared less for superstition and more for the practical realities of the stable, but I had thought for a moment that the gods might have touched the choice." Siger was angry now, his voice sharp and his ears pricked forward. Regi could not blame him. Having a pebafri named for the Lady of poisons in the stable would have seemed sign to anyone, including Regi. He could not blame Siger for what appeared a rational assumption. Blaming Siger was no more logical than blaming the entire culture for encouraging Kowri to see the gods' hands in such coincidence.

"What steps have you taken to locate Dante?"

After a brief moment of continued ire, Siger relaxed, and his next words carried the gentler tones of appeasement. "The animal I gave him to ride was a slow beast, and unlikely to panic." He huffed. "It is equally unlikely to hurry in any direction no matter how much his rider urges him. No doubt we shall find Dante somewhere near the original accident. We have only to go back and spread out until we can locate both."

"I will go with you," Regi said. Peaches exploded into a chitter of fury, quills rattling and her short claws digging into the skin of Regi's shoulder. Siger's eyes grew wide, and he stared at Peaches with the sort of horror a Coalition member might stare at a piece of unexploded ordinance that they unexpectedly found in their path.

"You should stay here and coordinate communication between the searchers and the temple," Siger said. "An exalted's call, your call, will receive priority if we have need of medical assistance, so having you relay any requests would prove helpful." While the request appeared reasonable, Peaches remained adamant in her fury. Her quills rattled and she sat on her haunches, her poor balance making her front legs kick the air. Regi held up his hand encouraging her to step onto it, but her fury was too great to be placated. Something was wrong.

"I shall contact exalted Alb and exalted Sibja to request their assistance." Peaches climbed into Regi's hand, gripping his middle three fingers as Regi walked back toward the road. He wished some privacy to speak with the other exalteds.

Behind him Siger called out, "They cannot help with the search. That will require riders atop pebafri, and exalted Alb is old enough that her bones would rattle apart if she sat on one. She could get hurt."

Regi ignored Siger's protest and signaled his communicator to call the women. Sibja answered first, and Dante summarized the situation and his growing concern given Peaches' state of agitation. Halfway through, Alb joined the call. When Regi attempted to begin his story again, she interrupted him.

"I have heard enough to know that Dante is likely in trouble," she said. "Will his god intervene?"

Dante had spoken very little of his god. Regi did not even know if his god was the one who had commanded so many of the humans to worship no god before him. Regi had been so concerned about his own theological problems that he had neglected to seek out information which he now needed. "I am unsure. I know the temple has not yet made any decision regarding the outsiders, but the Lady Divashi's hand is in evidence through her dop's behavior. We should meet at the cold weather temple to see if exalted Nawr has some insight. I have a hover and I can return to the temple quickly."

"I do not recommend it," Alb said. "If, by chance, Dante has suffered an accident, many exalteds might see that as proof of the gods' displeasure. We should not reveal this to anyone besides those who already know."

"But if the gods are moving, then surely the temple is the proper place for us to be," Regi said.

"If the gods are moving, yes," said Alb. "However, you and I know that the will of the gods is difficult to understand, and exalteds are no different from any other sapient creature. They will interpret signs in a way that best matches beliefs they already hold. If the Lady Divashi leads you to the protection of Dante, we would best serve the Lady by not allowing too many Kowri to know the truth."

As much as her words were logical, Regi chafed under her suggestion. When he'd been a child, he had family to support him. As an adult, he could turn to his shipmates, although the amount of support he'd received had been inversely proportional to how prejudiced they were against his species. But now he felt he had no support. Vk and Ter would help if they could, but with the ship grounded on a Kowri world, they had no ability to assist.

He wanted to run to the temple like a child seeking a parent's arms. He wanted someone to reassure him that he could trust his gods and the fellow creatures who were helping him. However, Alb was right that the political situation was too uncertain to toss more uncertainty into the milieu.

He turned to the stables—the staff rushing to their pebafri and Siger calling out commands. The Lady Divashi's Brown stood in the shade of the stable, a tuft of grass sticking outside the side of her mouth as she chewed. After a second, the pebafri looked at Regi.

No. That would be stupid. Regi had not been on a pebafri in ten years, and even when he had ridden, he had never been a good rider. He had no business on a beast not yet used to the saddle.

And yet, like Siger, he was infected with his people's belief in signs.

"I need to find Dante," Regi said when he realized the communicator was still active. He disconnected and headed toward the giant beast. This was the worst idea he'd had in a long time, but if the Lady Divashi watched out for him, maybe Lady Divashi's Brown would throw Regi off on the same slope where Dante had lost control of his pebafri.

Chapter Ten

The rest of the riders were still coordinating their search areas when Regi climbed the fence and used it to swing up onto the animal's back. "What are you doing on that beast?" Siger asked

"As you said, having a pebafri named after the Lady Divashi seems too significant to ignore," Regi said with more confidence than he felt. Most male pebafri were smaller than their female counterparts, even if they were more aggressive. Lady Divashi's Brown stamped his feet and swung his head about in search of a target for his horn, but unlike most males, he was huge—larger than all but one of the other pebafri in the corral.

"That is the thinking that caused me to be on an unstable pebafri when the outsider required assistance," Siger said with frustration and perhaps self-hate coloring his tone. "This is my stable and I am telling you to get off that pebafri."

Regi had never thrown his title about, not even when the other exalteds were being so irrational that all he wanted to do was explain to them the depths of their stupidity. However, Regi stared straight at Siger with all the contempt he could muster. "I am an exalted. Are you suggesting that I am incapable of making my own interpretations of my god's intentions?"

Siger opened his mouth, closed it, and then tilted his ears so far back that it was clear that he would've laid them against his skull were Kowri capable of doing so. "That pebafri is mine. I will not have my stable associated with the death of an exalted who was too foolish to understand that he had no business on an unbroken animal."

"I am an exalted of the cold-weather temple. I have walked among the most dangerous animals on the Kowri worlds, and they have seen me and acknowledged my god's hand guiding me. I may claim, in the name of the cold-weather temple, any resources the gods directed me to claim." Since Regi was not popular among the other exalteds, he was unsure at how they would feel about compensating Siger based on Regi's claim, but the calm with which Peaches watched this exchange convinced Regi that he was walking down the gods' own path.

Either that, or the Lady Divashi had been distracted by some other grain of sand in the universe and she no longer watched. Regi had to hope that was not the case, although every exalted knew the gods were fickle with their attention. Some exalteds were abandoned for so long that the stain of their god's touch faded, and with it the esteem of the sacred animals and their status. Gavd ship captains haunted the cold-weather temples both to prove their status and to place themselves in the line of their god's sight. A boring exalted of Gavd earned a demotion to a simple devotee who had once been touched, and god-touches were common enough.

Regi assumed his life provided suitable entertainment, but there was no way for Regi to know if his god watched at any given time, unless the Lady Divashi guided his steps with her usual subtlety, leading to more broken bones. Regi picked up the reins and kicked the pebafri's flanks. He burst into a lunging gait that made Peaches curse in her chittering voice and grab Regi's hair to keep from sliding down his back.

"I should go with you." Siger gathered up the reins of the largest of the pebafri remaining in the corral, a mare who was at least a hand-width taller than Goddess's Brown. Regi might have accepted an offer of escort, but Goddess's Brown muscles gathered in ominous warning. Regi gripped the animal's sides with his knees and held the front edge of the saddle before Goddess's Brown launched himself into the air and cleared most of the corral fence. He hit the top of rail, causing the wood to crack with a sound like a percussion weapon before the pieces clattered to the ground.

Regi was concerned about whether the animal was injured, but Lady Divashi's Brown never broke stride. He careened down walkways while pedestrians frowned at Regi, no doubt disapproving of his choice to ride within town proper. Unfortunately, Regi had very little control. However, as minutes passed, Regi realized that he was not in immediate danger of falling off and breaking his neck. He gathered up the reins and pretended that he had some control. When Thrice Mountain was on his immediate left, Regi tried to rein the pebafri toward it, but Goddess's Brown ignored him. If anything, he ran faster.

"Lady Divashi, Lord Gavd, if this is merely an untamed pebafri who is unwilling to return to the trail where he saw another fall, please send me some sign or help me get off this creature's back, preferably without breaking any more bones that would make it impossible to do your work." Regi kept his prayers soft so that others would not hear. For so long he had eschewed prayer, so it felt impious to call on the gods now when he needed their assistance. However, he had little choice if he hoped to reach Dante in time.

Kowri worlds were not safe. One could walk through a town, assuming one avoided the greed or malice of other Kowri, and those sins were more easily avoided than on a hundred other worlds Regi had visited. But outside the towns and cities and sprawling ports with their shipyards, Kowri worlds were filled with predators who maintained their dominion over the planet. Children were not encouraged to explore, and when school-aged younglings learned biology and ecology, they went into these wilderness areas only under supervision.

Regi had his anelace and his weapon. He had no doubt Siger also carried both. But Dante had no weapon, no knowledge of local flora or fauna, and while Dante had an affinity for god-touched animals, showing enough skill on the pebafri that Siger had agreed to lead him on a trail, the animals on the home worlds were not gods-touched. They were killers who would defend their territories and their mates and their offspring with claw and fang.

Regi wondered if Dante was as prejudiced as other outsiders in fearing larger animals more than small. If so edvidas or gibuks would kill him before any predator had the opportunity.

Neither god answered his prayer, which could suggest they guided the pebafri or Regi had strayed so far from the path they had set out that the gods no longer watched him. Either meant that Regi was trapped until Lady Divashi's Brown slowed long enough for him to dismount without risking his bones.

After passing a tall house with balconies adorning the corners, the animal turned toward the wilderness. This was the densest part of the local forest. The proximity of the cold-weather temple meant that the most poisonous and dangerous creatures were found in this sector. And while those creatures touched by a god were unlikely to kill without provocation, untouched animals would follow their brethren. Gavd might touch a pebafri, but her herd with their sharp hoofs and horns would follow her into the area.

Lady Divashi's Brown waded through hip-tall weeds before reaching the forest proper where shade strangled the worst of the undergrowth. The eerie cry of a frim cut the air, and the creature's flock answered until the undulating shrieks filled the air. Glorious. The situation grew worse with every turn, which is why Regi suspected the first blessing of the gods was well and truly at work.

Chapter Eleven

Dante let out a string of profanity that would've sent his grandmother searching for a bar of soap. He stood and brushed off his pants and eyed the steep slope that he had failed—once again—to ascend. He'd clambered up steeper ground in his youth, but either the rocks here were looser or Dante was getting old. Every time he thought he had found a hand hold, he would slide to the bottom again. His hands were scraped raw, and his hip ached from the earlier fall.

Dante glared at the slope before turning his attention to the rest of his surroundings. He possessed a good sense of direction, and this cut in the ground was between him and that town. So he needed to find a way around it. He looked towards the sky. "Lady Divashi, if you keep flinging me back to the bottom of this hill, I don't mind telling you that I am getting a little aggravated with your high-handedness."

Dante wondered whether his grandmother would've considered his words a prayer. Probably. But then she would've been so scandalized by his recent spate of cursing that she wouldn't have had any more room for additional horror.

Muttering about interfering women, Dante studied the flat ground to the left and right. Since he had no idea where he was going and had never seen an aerial picture that would have at least given him a general sense of geography, Dante chose right at random. "I assume if you disapprove, you will do something." Dante started down the sandy path. The trail had been formed by running water, Broken tree limbs and debris gathered at each bend in the path, but the same water had carved a trail for him to follow. Of course, he still had to navigate the uneven ground and rocks that littered the way. After months of walking the smooth corridors of the ship, his ankles protested the workout.

"You know, I've no intention of worshiping you. At best, you're an annoying busybody who is always trying to tell other people how to live their life. When I lived in Houston, I had a neighbor like you," Dante told the sky. He didn't expect anyone was listening, but wildlife didn't like to be startled. Making noise was the best way to ensure that he didn't interrupt some wildcat's dinner or startle baby wild pigs so that their screams called the adults to attack. The rule on a trail was that if you wanted to see wildlife, you kept quiet, and if you wanted to avoid wildlife, you acted like some city tourists who talked at a volume that would only be appropriate when trying to have a conversation with someone on the opposite side of a crowded subway.

So Dante did his best to imitate a tourist.

"I bet Regi thinks that you made sure I was out alone on the ranch that night, and that you picked me because your hedgehogs needed someone to love them. Well, I don't mind loving your hedgehogs because they are sweet creatures, but if I ever get evidence that you conspired with those assholes to take me off Earth, I will figure out a way to ascend to whatever dimension you live in, and I will kick your ass so hard that you won't sit for a month." That threat was more effective when the person he was threatening had a corporeal butt. "Screwing with people's lives is not acceptable behavior." That had always been his grandmother's most condemning phrase. If you insulted guest or kissed a boy in front of others, she pulled out the not-acceptable-behavior line. Dante knew she had been trying to protect him, but it still rankled.

"At least ask if people want your help. The Kowri appreciate your help, and you have guided them do some amazing stuff. I wish humans had been able to reach space without having to strip every corner of the planet to get there." In his lifetime, Dante had seen the ranch halve and halve again because the value of land and the taxes attached to it had risen so much. As more land became unusable from overmining and rising water, it seemed like there was very little space for the life Dante had grown up loving. The only thing saving the ranch was the tourists. Rich people valued rare experiences, and riding on an open range was becoming an exotic adventure.

Right after high school, Dante had moved to Montana to study Equine Science. That was the last part of the country that had huge tracks of untouched land. He'd wanted open spaces without the shadows of civilization creeping in with every distant blast of a semi horn. But the minute the first winter storm had hit the dorm rooms with such fury that the walls shook, he had called his father. He might hate his dad, but the man had the connections and the money to get Dante out of a bad situation of his own making.

"Why couldn't you break the pirate's ship so they had to land?" Dante asked the sky as he trudged down the dry creek bed. "Earth could have reverse engineered their engines and gotten a jumpstart on technology we needed to get out of the solar system. At the same time, your dops could have found a new home. Yeah, my people probably would've put them in a zoo, but they would put them in a nice zoo. My people are better to animals than they are to each other. Usually." Dante grimaced and he thought about the work he had done with the horse rescue. People who didn't have space for horses often insisted on keeping them because the animals were a huge part of Texas culture. And in Texas, culture mattered more than the law. "My people are good with exotic animals they see as having value. Any zoo with an alien animal exhibit would've made some damn good money."

"Maybe you didn't think about that. Maybe you're as fallible as the people down here—only with a different perspective." Or maybe Divashi didn't trust humans. Dante could hardly blame her. Then again, Kowri weren't better. Between the politics at the temple and

Siger's backstabbing, Dante was damn disappointed in them. They weren't the monsters the Coalition made them out to be, but they were disappointingly ordinary on the moral front. Dante had nursed some childish hope that when he met aliens, they would be better.

Dante heard some large creature crashing through the brush on the high ground above the creek bed. He looked around for a sturdy branch that he could use as a weapon and cursed himself for not doing that earlier. There was a lack of downed branches in the immediate area. He considered turning and running back to the nearest bend in the creek bed where there had been a pile up of tree litter, but he didn't want to turn his back on a potential predator, and he didn't want to run on rocky ground. The first was an invitation to get chased and the second was a near guarantee that he would twist an ankle if not break one.

So instead he ripped a whippy little branch off an overhanging limb and prayed that he could bluff whatever monster was about to accost him.

"Dammit! Stop, you gods' cursed beast."

Dante let his hand fall to his side and called out, "Hello? Hello! I need some help down here."

"Dante?" Incredulity came through the translator fine.

A great crashing through the brush presaged Regi tumbling to the bottom of the slope. He sat in the rocky creek bed with a dazed expression and his fur so poofed that he resembled a fuzzy teddy bear. Dante decided not to share that observation.

With relief so great that it made his knees weak running through him, Dante closed the distance between them. "Thank God. I didn't think anyone would find me before one of these cold-weather predators you keep talking about ate me."

Regi rubbed his hand over his face and his fur settled; however, he didn't respond.

Dante crouched down next to him. "Are you okay?"

"What are the parameters of 'okay'?" Regi asked, which was not a reassuring question.

"If you need a doctor, you're not."

Regi nodded with deliberate, slow movements. "I do not need a doctor for any effects of that fall. I am not okay in my frustration towards certain individuals. I may need a doctor of Ean's ilk to release negative emotions that are leading me toward antisocial behaviors."

Dante silently translated that to Regi being pissed at Siger. Or Divashi. Regi's goddess did provide more than her share of bad luck. But, since Regi's bad luck had led him to find Dante in the middle of the wilderness, Dante was Team Divashi this time. Given his earlier rant, that was hypocritical, but Dante was fine with embracing his own selfish needs.

"I'm shocked you found me. I thought Siger's murder plot would work." Dante stood and offered Regi his hand.

Halfway through reaching for it, Regi froze. "What do you say Siger possessed?"

"He didn't possess anything, but he did orchestrate a murder plot. That's what we call it when someone intentionally organizes events to try to kill someone else."

"Kowri are not above corporeal greed or sin. I understand the concept of murder plot and that is one of the crimes that followers of Gavd are charged with investigating. However, why do you believe Siger attempted to murder you?"

"He attacked me and the pebafri I was riding while shouting things about how Gavd was the true God and Divashi was evil and a whole bunch of other bullshit I didn't catch since I was trying to avoid death." Regi mouthed the word *bullshit* as if he couldn't quite understand it. That was fair, he probably couldn't. Dante had no doubt Kowri, and every other species cursed in their own language, but the translator skipped those words.

"At the stables, Siger is coordinating the search for you. He said your pebafri stepped badly." Regi put his hand in Dante's, but he hauled most of his own weight up, not relying on Dante to provide a counterbalance.

"My pebafri stepped badly after he struck both of us with a whip. I don't know whether it was my years in the saddle or the Lady Divashi who kept me from bashing my brains out on the way down the slope." Dante grimaced. "Maybe both." He had seen less serious falls result in broken necks or cracked skulls. Siger had not offered a helmet, and Dante hadn't asked for one because he had trusted his own ability to stay in the saddle. Even without the murder plot, that had been reckless given that he didn't have experience with pebafri.

Regi's ears were back. "That complicates matters. I had no idea he was a Gavd monotheist. That belief doesn't even make sense to me. If Gavd is the only god or the only god that matters, then why do the other gods have power?" Regi's eyes widened. "Not that I am casting aspersions on your people's religious beliefs."

"Don't worry about that. If we ever get back to Earth, my people will be casting lots of aspersions. They will probably tell you that your gods are another alien species, and one that has been created by their God since their God is above all." Dante checked Regi's walk, searching for any sign he was injured. The fall had not been a pleasant one. However, he seemed fine, although his fur was so full of dust that his stripes were half-hidden by a layer of gray.

"That would be a fascinating theological discussion," Regi said.

"I believe the translator has miss-translated horrific shit storm," Dante corrected him.

Regi flashed him a grin. "Let's call for assistance, and then we can discuss the vagaries of theology." He pulled out his communicator and asked for any follower of Gavd who could provide rescue. The communicator produced static and pops, but no voice came through. Regi had alarm in his gaze as he repeated the request.

"Did you break it on the way down?"

Regi grimaced. "Perhaps, which is a striking piece of irony."

That comment made very little sense to Dante, but since Regi was busy pulling the cover off the communicator, Dante found the nearest non-jagged boulder and perched on it. It gave him a chance to stretch his ankles.

"I don't see any physical damage, but I don't have equipment to examine the smaller details." Regi snapped the back on. "Instead of providing rescue, unfortunately I may have simply provided a traveling companion as we will both need to walk back to town."

"I don't mind a traveling companion at all, especially if you're armed. I don't suppose you have a weapon you could loan me."

For long seconds, Regi studied him, as though trying to parse some poorly translated message, his eyes wide and the hair at the edges of his eyes standing on end in a way that made him look alarmed. "Why would you need a weapon? Why would I need a weapon?"

Now Dante fell silent as shock stalled his brain. He had never thought of Regi as stupid, but that statement came near it. "Siger tried to kill me." That was more than enough reason to desire a weapon.

Regi's features smoothed as his worry drained away. "He has taken riders miles off course to search for you."

"He could double back to finish killing me."

Regi began studying the path where the Lady Divashi had dumped them. Either that or Siger had dumped Dante here and she had sent Regi along after him. "If Siger were to leave the rescue, many would ask why. Since he carries a new communicator, many would follow if he attempted to leave."

"Communicators can be used as trackers? Why didn't they track the riding path he took us on?" Dante did not understand how these people could have phenomenal technological advances and still have these huge blind spots.

"He left his phone behind on the initial ride, but they are, no doubt, tracking him now. Such surveillance of every Kowri would require obscene amounts of storage. The temple only tracks an individual if something remarkable is going on. Siger losing an outsider who is central to a temple debate is remarkable enough that others will watch him. The local predators are far more significant a danger." Regi slapped his hands together, dislodging a significant amount of dust from the fur of his arms.

Dante had very little faith in the Kowri people or Regi's ability to predict their behavior, but a faint chittering derailed his thoughts. "Is that a dop?" Dante had no doubt that wild dops were dangerous. They would have all the poison of the dops on the ship without being used to handling.

"Peaches!" Regi called.

"Peaches? You dropped my Peaches down a slope?" Horror washed through Dante, and he scrambled up the loose bank toward the unhappy chittering. As he climbed, Dante crooned, "*Chee chee chee chee chee.* Come on Peaches. *Chee chee chee.*"

"She chose to come with me," Regi said from the bottom of the slope. He wasn't trying to climb up after Dante, but then for all his vigorous efforts, Dante was only five or six feet above the creek bed. This soil was far too loose for climbing. However, Dante wouldn't abandon his favorite dop—the one who had chosen to stay with him when the others had all run for freedom.

"You dropped her somewhere up here."

"I was thrown from the back of a rearing pebafri. She suffered no more than I have. In addition, she is god-touched. One does not tell a god-touched creature where to go."

Dante spared one cranky look over his shoulder before he focused on the slope in front of him. He called out again, and this time the chittering was much louder. A small pink nose appeared through a tangle of brittle branches. "Peaches!" Dante held out his hand, and she waddled into it so he could pull her close. He stroked her quills to make sure they were all lying flat before he flipped her over onto her back to check for injuries. Four tiny paws kicked the air and the prehensile tail she kept rolled up under her belly stretched up towards Dante. Dante righted her and held her close enough for her to climb up his shirt.

"I won't trust you with my dops again." Dante slid back down the slope.

"They are the Lady Divashi's dops. And she trusts both of us with them because Peaches insisted on coming."

Dante studied Regi. For all his dismissive words, his ears were lowered. "I will forgive you because you believed you were searching for a missing person, not investigating a murder plot, but next time, I do not want my critters in the middle of danger." Dante was serious about that. Peaches was the queen of the ship, and her company had saved him from insanity more than once. After David had punched one of the slavers in search of a quick death—one he'd found at the Styl's hands—Dante had considered doing the same. Sitting with Peaches playing on his lap had been the only thread of sanity that had kept him from suicide.

"I am rather more concerned that you are in the middle of danger," Regi countered.

"I'm not the one to worry about."

Regi cocked his head. "I do not understand the implications of that statement. Who else would I worry about?"

"Siger," Dante said, his voice flat. "I have plans for that bastard, plans that involve his eternal humiliation if not his death. I wouldn't mind his death."

"Dante." Regi rested his hand on Dante's arm. "I regret this, but few Kowri would take the word of an outsider against someone as established as Siger."

Dante grinned. "Then we convince them. After all, the guy is a Gavd monotheist. If he is willing to be this crazy in support of his beliefs, don't you think he's done other crazy shit? He's done something we can use to make him eternally regret trying to kill me. And Peaches." Dante stroked her quills and she shivered them until they made a rattling noise.

"I begin to doubt your sanity," Regi said with a weary sigh.

"My sanity has been in doubt for a long time. But then, I followed you into a radioactive engine, and it worked out. I'm willing to bet that if we put our minds to making Siger miserable, we can find a way. After all, this feels a lot like a god's first blessing," Dante pointed out. Not one but both had been thrown off pebafri in the middle of nowhere. Based on the stories Regi had told, that did feel like something the gods would do.

"Are you saying you trust the gods to show you a path, one you plan to follow?" Regi's eyes grew wide with shock.

"I'm saying I know how to take advantage of any opportunity that appears, god-given or not." And if necessary, Dante had a little friend with very poisonous quills. Dante remembered how Carlos had died. He'd aggravated one of the smaller dops, poking it until the docile creature had shot a half dozen quills into Carlos's hand. Within an hour, his hand was swollen, and red tracks marked the inside of his arm like some sort of zombie make up. An hour after that, he'd started throwing up blood. He'd died screaming in pain. Carlos been a good man who hadn't been able to face one more day as a slave, and he'd chosen the only escape he could see. He deserved better.

Siger didn't.

Chapter Twelve

"What are you trying to do?" Dante asked.

Regi looked up from his communicator to find Dante watching him from several lengths ahead. "The communication network has separate channels for terrestrial and aeroterrestrial networks. I know I am unable to access the aeroterrestrial network, but I hope that as we get closer to town, that I can pick up a terrestrial signal and request assistance."

"So satellites versus telephone wires?"

Regi struggled with the images provided by the translator. "Perhaps. Technology and the names of animals rarely translate well. That is one reason why the Coalition employs linguists. When attempting to contact a new species or navigate nuanced issues of policy, one does not want to rely on a translator program."

Dante held onto a low hanging branch to provide balance as he climbed over a tumble of rocks. Peaches clung to the collar of his shirt and chittered her disapproval with the amount of jostling she was enduring. That tone would have worried Regi, but Dante seemed unbothered by having a frustrated dop near his face. "I discovered that when I was taking French."

"French?" The term had not translated at all.

"My language is English. French is another one of the languages spoken on my planet. When I was in school, I had the brilliant idea of using a translator program instead of doing my homework. It didn't end well for me."

Regi could imagine the failures a translation program would generate without access to the universal translation programming with the thousands of planetary languages. "All of us are great fools when we are still young enough to be in school."

"I can't imagine you being stupid."

"I was," Regi assured him. "My parents would, no doubt, love to share stories of my foolishness, which lasted well beyond my school years." Looking back, he could admit his decision to leave the Empire had been fueled in part by his ridiculous assumption that Gavd's rejection of his petition was a humiliating defeat. Sometimes Regi suspected that he had chosen Poque as his new patron only because no one expected her to give any sign of favor. Therefore, his failure to earn such a sign did not impugn his abilities.

Dante interrupted his musings. "My father would have insisted I was a fool all the way up to the day that I disappeared. Now he gets the advantage of being a family man without the inconvenience of having me around to damage his reputation."

Regi did not know how huuman parenting worked, but he imagined Dante's father would be happy to have a child returned, even if he did not approve of Dante's choices. Regi assumed that was how his own parents would react, and he assumed most parents were the same. However, he empathized with Dante's trepidation at the idea of reestablishing communication with his father. Regi felt the same, except he had left behind three disappointed parents. He assumed word of his return had reached them, so Regi feared he would have to contend with parental disapproval far sooner than Dante would.

The Empire had better communication networks and faster engines than the Coalition, but technology had limits, and their arrival would depend on whether some god-given task distracted his mother. It usually did. "Did you study language as your vocation?" Regi asked. He found it discomforting to have a conversation without looking at the other party involved, but he had already fallen in the loose rocks, so he kept his gaze focused on his feet.

Dante laughed. "I barely survived high school French. And I grew up in Texas and can't speak more than a spattering of Spanglish, so we can safely say that language is not my strength."

Huumans must take education seriously to speak of seeking to survive a course of study. "What did you study?" Regi knew he had been a tender of animals of sorts, but he did not know if that had been his chosen vocation.

"I have an Associates in equine studies."

"That did not translate." The slavers had not spoken to their slaves often enough for the translator function to identify enough target language to work well.

They were climbing a small swell in the ground, and Dante remained silent as he clambered over a boulder that some flood had deposited on the creek bed. The passage was growing more difficult to navigate, but unless Regi could find a signal and communicate their need for transportation, they didn't have any choice other than to continue walking. Dante didn't answer until they were on the far side of the obstruction. "I studied how to take care of horses, recognize horse diseases, design diets, and judge quality. That sort of stuff."

"You are the huuman equivalent of Siger without the radical religious beliefs that inspire murder," Regi summarized.

This time Dante's laugh was more musical. "I have radical beliefs, but none about religion. I try to avoid the topic. I assume you studied something relevant to security."

"I spent my temple years studying criminal behavior."

Dante glanced back at him. "Temple years?"

Regi held up four fingers. "Mothers' years, fathers' years, temple years, own years."

Dante gave a great sigh and chose a flat boulder to sit on. Peaches climbed down his arm and shook out her quills while Dante propped a foot on an adjacent rock. "Are those stages of childhood?" he asked.

Regi held up his first finger "Mothers' years. The first six years of life, a Kowri stays with his mother."

"Do mothers stay home?"

Regi was confused into silence. Some days huuman culture felt like a mirror of Kowri in ways Regi had never experienced. Other days Regi could not comprehend the turns Dante's mind took. "Why would they stay home?"

Dante frowned, an expression Regi was learning to associate with confusion. "Because you said their kids stayed with them."

"Children stay with mothers as mothers continue their work. I attended many difficult pregnancies because my mother was an exalted of Otutha."

"Oh." Dante frowned; he had not expected such an answer. But Regi could not imagine how a culture could function if a third of workers could vanish from productive work at any given time, or how the gods would react if Kowri decided to avoid life while raising children. Given that huuman culture had only two genders, they might have an even higher percentage of those who bore young. "That must have made it hard on your mother," Dante concluded.

It probably had, but given Regi's difficult relationship with his mother and her goddess, Regi had not looked at it from her point of view. As an adult, he could not imagine how he would handle Divashi's attention while having a child. "My mother did her best, but as a child, I often believed her best was inadequate," he admitted.

Dante snorted. "My father managed to be inadequate without a god interfering with his life. At least your mother had a good excuse."

Regi would rather avoid discussions of his own difficult family relationships, especially since those problems were likely to appear if

Regi could not get off this planet in a few sets of days. "Did other huumans judge your father inadequate?"

Dante pulled his shoe off and rubbed his foot. Regi chose a rock on which to sit, but he feared that if he removed his shoes, his feet would hurt even more when he had to walk again. He wished his communicator could find a signal, but when he checked it, he was still without access to the network.

"My father..." Dante studied his foot for a moment before continuing to rub it. "My people don't have exalteds. We elect people to represent us. My father is one of those elected. He holds a position called senator." He stopped again.

Regi shifted to avoid an uncomfortable protrusion on his chosen boulder. "Many planets choose leaders that way. It is one of the most common governmental structures."

"That's a little sad. I had hoped aliens would have a better solution."

That surprised Regi. Individuals who came from democratic structures exhibited much more satisfaction with their government than those like the Styl with challenge-based meritocracies or inherited positions like the Bewiio. "What is your concern with that form of government?"

For a long time, Dante sat in silence. "It's a popularity contest," he said. "My father will do anything to be popular, and that means he doesn't care about family or doing what's right. He cares about having people like him. After my mother died, my father handed me over to my grandmother to raise because he didn't want me to infect him with social outcastedness."

"Grand mother? A supervisor of mothers?" Regi guessed.

"Um, no. A grandmother is the mother of one of a person's parents. She was my mother's mother."

"Ah." The term "*grand*" was used metaphorically in this situation. "I knew the parents of each of my parents, but such do not have a unique relationship to a child. It is rare for all three parents to be judged inadequate to the task of raising a child at the same time, but when such happens, another who is of the same age as the parent will take in the child."

"Foster parents. We have those too, but my father makes himself popular by making people believe he is good at everything."

Regi was confused. "Then how could he justify giving your mother's years to the mother of your mother?"

"I was older than that. I was twelve when my mother was killed."

"So you had just entered your temple years." Those were difficult years for any sentient creature, but if huumans were like Kowri, the social awkwardness of those specific years was painful. Temple years were a difficult time of making one's own choices and leaving parents behind for the first time, and yet making a rich variety of mistakes on such a wide range of topics that one could only suffer humiliation at the memory. Regi hoped huumans had an easier transition to adulthood.

"My dad... he played up the grieving widower role. He rode that publicity right into office. Anyway, that topic is even more depressing than your goddess's shitty habit of dropping us in the middle of some disaster and expecting us to survive on our own." Dante turned his face toward the sky. "You are a horrible, horrible woman."

Horror gripped Regi's heart, but Divashi chose not to react. Regi hoped he was wrong about Dante having her attention or she would take offense at some point.

"So, temple years. Twelve to how old?" The sentence structure was awkward, but Regi understood the general meaning.

"We are in our temple years from twelve to eighteen, and we choose a temple—cold season, growing season or harvest season, and study the occupations associated with that temple. Many will move from one temple to another and one vocation to another. However, I spent that set of years working toward becoming a follower of Gavd. I was determined that I should solve crimes and ensure justice on each planet I visited." Now Regi was embarrassed about his misplaced enthusiasm.

"Then you get a job at eighteen?"

"Then we have own years," Regi corrected him. "We work in professions that align with our chosen goals. The temple pays our salary as we develop our skills to the point that others may find value in hiring us."

"So six years of schooling and six years of internship. So, twelve years of education. I guess we're not that far off, although that would put you at twenty-four before you're finished. And how many years have you worked for the Coalition?"

Regi had to count back the years in each of his various roles to figure an answer. "Almost a two set."

"Two set?"

"Almost twelve," Regi clarified. Being back amongst Kowri, it was easy to return to old habits of thinking.

"So, you're thirty-five?" Dante whistled, a shrill sound that resembled the hunting call of the betiin bird. "You're an old man."

"I have used roughly one-quarter of the years allotted to me as a Kowri. How many years are huumans, given that you believe thirty-five is old?" Regi had only recently begun thinking of himself as well established in his working years. He had heard Ter argue vociferously and with great passion that any creature under a half-century was too young for any degree of responsibility.

"A few less than you. Most of us live between eighty and a hundred years. But I'm only twenty, so thirty-five feels pretty old to me."

"Twenty? You have not yet finished four sets of years?" Regi must have misheard, or the translation must have been mistaken.

"Nope. I'm in my fourth," Dante said. He slid his foot back into his shoe with a grimace that suggested he regretted having removed it.

He had only begun the fourth set. He should be under the direction of a temple, exploring the career options before choosing one. Regi understood that his discomfort was illogical given that different species matured at different rates, but that knowledge did not blunt his feelings. "At that age, are you considered fully mature?"

"Yep." With a sigh, Dante stood. His grimace deepened into something that hinted at pain. "Well, except for drinking, but trust me, everyone in Texas ignores the legal drinking age. And by every other measure, I'm an adult."

"But you are still legally limited by your lack of years?" Regi clarified. This issue was of far more import than Dante's casual attitude suggested. Unless the translator had misfunctioned, the slavers had taken an individual who was not yet matured by the laws of their own people.

Dante studied him, one eye more open than the other and the hair above one eye drawn downward. "I guess so, but eighteen is an adult for everything except drinking."

"But the pirates chose to enslave someone too young to be unrestricted by age." Regi would amend his reports to include that detail. That would earn any pirates they could arrest additional years of punishment. At this point, the only way to make their crime worse would be if huumans were a vernal species, but they owned two planets, so that charge could not be levied against them. "Were any of the other huumans too young to be fully unrestricted?"

Dante answered slowly. "One. Sophie—the one who died in an airlock when the oxygen was evacuated. She was eighteen."

Eighteen. Had she been Kowri, she would have been completing her temple set of years. Regi would amend his reports to include the pirates' participation in the death of one not yet of full maturity. Now he needed to find some captain willing to pursue the pirates on behalf of Divashi. The Coalition had a policy of arresting and pursuing criminals only when their ships were within sight of established lanes and their communication networks. Regi felt a burning need to pursue these monsters to whatever dark hole they had chosen to hide in and rip them from reality.

"She wanted to be a doctor," Dante said. "She should have been home studying for her freshman year of college, but her car broke down in the middle of nowhere and the slavers grabbed her. She was a kid. She'd had two good parents who sheltered her from everything, so all of us tried to help her through the hard days." Dante's words came slower, and he rubbed his face.

"Both of you deserved to be sheltered. Neither of you was fully entrenched in adulthood. And all the slaves deserved to be rescued from such horrific conditions." Regi got up and came to Dante's side, capturing one of Dante's slender hands in his. "I pledge on my honor that I will do everything I can to find the rest of the pirates and either return them to Coalition or Empire space for punishment or destroy their ships, so they die screaming in the black of space with no one to mourn them." For long seconds, they stared at each other. Perhaps it was arrogance, but Regi felt as if fate watched, twining the threads of their lives together as they gazed at one another. Too many people had failed this brave huuman, and Regi would not add his name to that list. Near them, Peaches sat with one leg up in the air as she cleaned her genitals without a care for the solemnity of the moment.

"That's dramatic," Dante said. "Why are you so angry now?"

"I had not realized that you were in your youth or that the one who died had not yet reached maturity."

"I'm an adult. I don't need you looking at me like I'm a child."

"You are not a child, but even by your own people's reckoning, you are not an unrestricted adult."

"Only when it comes to mind-altering substances. I am an adult in every way that matters, and even when it comes to alcohol, no one will give me grief about my age unless they hate my father and want to make life difficult for him by making me look bad. I know that one firsthand. And I handled slavery a whole lot better than a couple of the older folks. So lay the fur back down and stop looking at me like I'm a five-year-old who got snatched away from his home."

Regi had not realized that the fur along his arms was standing on end. He took a moment to smooth it back down, the long strokes of his palm soothing his nerves. Dante reached out and rested his hand against Regi's forearm for a second, and they again studied each other.

"I appreciate your anger because someone must stop those pirates, but I survived. I don't need you to ride to my rescue. So you hunt those bastards down for Richard who was the kindest man I ever knew. He taught history at Kansas State University. You do it for David whose neck was snapped by that Styl bastard. You do it for Sophie who died of radiation, and Carlos who aggravated one of the dops until the creature finally gave him what he wanted and drove a poison quill into his hand. You hunt them down for the poor bastard who went out a decompression lock without ever giving the rest of us his name. But I survived. Don't swear to hunt them for my sake."

Regi studied Dante's features, sure he would see some sign that Dante spoke out of a need to maintain some ephemeral sense of power. However, confidence and surety shone from his eyes. "You are a brave man."

"I'm a practical one," Dante said.

Regi would have argued, only his communicator chirped as it found an associated network connection. Regi pulled it from his pocket, joy staining his feelings as he turned it on. The communicator identified Alb as his caller, and Regi answered with a prayer of thanks for all the gods of each season.

"Regi a'Divashi, I have tried calling you many times," she said.

"My communicator is broken. I thought we would have to walk the entire distance to town, but the second blessing of the gods has followed on the heels of the first." Regi was almost giddy with relief, but he realized his answer was cryptic when Alb allowed the silence to continue long enough to become awkward.

She asked, "Where are you? Siger reported that you disappeared on his most disagreeable pebafri."

"I did. I believed my goddess guided my actions, and that disagreeable pebafri has led me to Dante. I found him. Can you track my location?" Dante stood and scooped up Peaches before standing close enough that Regi could feel the heat of his body. No doubt he wished to hear both sides of the conversation.

"I can track your location, but I do not understand why you would be in that place."

"Lady Divashi led me here because Siger is leading the rescue teams in the wrong direction. He attacked Dante and left him out here to die. We need some followers of Gavd to retrieve us."

"Siger betrayed the outsider?" Alb's voice was small and horrified.

"He did. It was the luck of the gods and Divashi's hand that led me to find him."

"Siger?" Alb's voice had a dangerous lack of emotion. She sounded like Regi's mother when she was trying to hide her emotions. Regi would not wish to stand in Siger's place when the exalted Alb a'Oba caught up with him. Her tongue-lashing would make the punishments of Gavd that would follow seem tame by comparison, even if he suspected any legal punishment would be precluded by a lack of evidence other than Dante's testimony.

"Did Siger indicate whether he was working with any others?"

Regi looked to Dante, but he shook his head.

"He did not. However, he is motivated by a belief that Gavd is the only proper god to worship and that Divashi's touch is a corruption."

"Are you swearing that Siger a'Gavd is a monotheistic extremist?" The question carried danger. If a Kowri swore to a truth that was later proven false, he would bear the stigma and the financial penalty for his mistake. It would be better to avoid swearing until he had concrete evidence in his hand. However, Regi trusted Dante's word in this.

"I am," he said with confidence.

"Such individuals rarely work alone. They exist in shadow temples organized in sheds and basements," Alb said. "We must move slowly, especially since there are exalteds of Gavd who speak against allowing the outsiders to return home. I had not thought a follower if Gavd capable of unprovoked violence, but the times are violent and Kowri are reacting in kind."

Regi traded concerned looks with Dante. She seemed to imply that they couldn't trust any follower of Gavd, not even the great god's exalteds. The thought inspired fear. "Individuals chosen by the god himself would not carry such heresy, would they??"

She sighed, her voice small as she answered, "I do not know. I fear, and that is enough to make me want to walk quietly. But I am an exalted of Oba, and I know the stories of many Kowri. I will use that knowledge to call those who are more favorable to our cause. However, others could reach you more easily were you not in such a narrow place. I am worried that if you continue to follow the path of the dry river, there are many places where a loose boulder could pose a danger or an unscrupulous Kowri could make a pair of deaths appear to be an accident of chance."

Regi's blood ran cold. He had faced many enemies in his years of fighting on Coalition ships. He had been present for the Veron Station Riots. He had boarded pirate ships and smugglers. He'd been in gun battles. But he had never thought to fear the duplicitousness of Kowri. However, Alb's words were logical. "What do you suggest?"

"Turn east out of that riverbed as soon as you can. You will soon reach the path that leads to the rear of the cold season temple. Follow that path in, and I will find followers of Gavd who I can trust. But you must turn off your communicator so others cannot track you. I have watched the network looking for you, and I hope my goddess guided me to see your signal before our enemies can locate you, but we cannot trust the gods to act when we are their hands. So turn off your communicator and trust that I will send you what help I can. Now take yourself off the communication network before the gods bless you beyond your ability to survive." She disconnected.

With his heart pounding and a sense of urgency, Regi pulled the back off the communicator and hit the switch to disable it.

"I guess we're walking," Dante said with a calm weariness that didn't seem to match the direness of the situation.

Regi sighed and considered the steep eastern bank of the riverbed. They would have to search out a place they could climb. "I guess we are," he agreed. They would walk and they would seek out the temple path, and when they got back to town, Regi planned to shove Siger's face into pebafri excrement. As long as Captain Cota did not see it, Regi could not be disciplined for following his instincts.

With a sigh, Dante began to walk, Peaches chittering her complaints as she clung to his shirt.

Chapter Thirteen

"We must be watchful as we navigate this area," Regi said.

Dante eyed the thinning trees with suspicion. This part of the planet resembled a literal walk in the park compared to climbing over flood-tossed boulders, but he assumed Regi would not have made that comment without some reason. "Why?"

"We are soon to reach the travelway for the cold weather temple."

Dante detoured around an arch of exposed tree roots higher than his hip as he tried to mentally decipher that statement, but it didn't make sense, even when Dante tried to think his way around the awkward phrases that the translator preferred. "What does that mean?"

Regi had taken lead, and he turned to face Dante. "Each of the three temples is connected to undeveloped territory to allow sacred animals free movement."

"Like parklands? Or is the land allowed to grow wild?" Dante appreciated untouched wilderness in theory, but in practice, that seemed to be a rather significant forest fire danger. Enormous trees towered overhead, blotting out the sun so only dappled patches of sunlight could penetrate when the wind stirred the leaves. If a fire started here, the land would turn into an apocalyptic inferno.

"It is generally untouched, but the trees will thin when we reach the actual passageway. It is the path animals will take if they are called by the gods to serve at the temple. Because there are so many animals walking along one path, the trees and foliage become thin."

Dante understood what Regi was saying. "The cold season temple has the most dangerous animals. Does that mean we're about to come along a game trail with the most dangerous animals on your planet?" Dante questioned Alb's motives if she was sending them into that kind of danger.

Regi held his hand down low before curling all six digits into a fist that he brought up to touch his temples with reverence. "The danger is far less for someone who is god-touched, and even less for an exalted. The sacred animals will sense that the gods have given us their favor, so any animal that is favored by the gods will recognize our right to be on this path."

That sounded suspiciously like Regi accepted that Dante was one of the exalteds. "Are you saying you believe Divashi has chosen me as much as you?" Dante wondered how that would play for his father's political supporters. Folks in Texas disapproved of gods other than the one in the local Baptist church.

"Alb, Sibja, and I agree that Divashi favors you. If anything, you are more in her favor since you cared for the dops when no one else did." Regi's gaze shifted to Peaches who surveyed her domain from atop Dante's shoulder.

Dante reached up and stroked the tender spot under her chin, and pleasure made her trill. "Okay, but if we are both touched by the gods and safe from sacred animals, why would this be dangerous?"

Regi leaned against a tree whose peeling white bark reminded Dante of a birch. "If Divashi touches a dop, it will move towards the temple. However, that dop's mate or offspring may follow without ever enjoying the goddess's touch."

Dante got it. "Even if a god-touched animal isn't dangerous, one of the others that come along with it could still kill us." Dante began walking again. He was exhausted but standing around did not move them toward rescue. Regi hurried to get in front. He had a charming overprotective streak that made Dante smile. Most of the time, his dating partners looked to get what they could out of Dante—either fame or money. They dropped Dante quick enough when they found he avoided the first, and his father wouldn't give him two nickels to rub together.

"Precisely. It is highly unlikely, and one of the gods would likely notice if creatures were contemplating evisceration, but one should never rely on the gods. They are great beings who must oversee grand works on a universal scale. It is entirely too easy for one who relies on the gods to suffer a cataclysmic accident while the gods have their gaze focused elsewhere. If the gods were able to watch all Kowri at all times, there would be no crime. And I assure you, my people do commit crimes."

"I think Siger proved that. I'm looking forward to punching him in the mouth." Dante engaged in some creative visualization of Siger's face twisted with shock right before Dante's fist hit it. Dante's old therapist would be proud of his ability to imagine the future he wanted. That hadn't been a skill he'd excelled at as a kid.

Regi puckered, an expression that Dante had learned to associate with grave concern. Punching a local would likely cause problems, so Dante changed the subject.

"You mentioned mothers' years and temple years, but you said something about having fathers' years in the middle, and you never explained what those were. You don't talk much about your fathers at all." Only after the words had escaped his mouth did it occur to Dante that this might be a sensitive subject. After all, he never liked talking about his mother. Her death had wounded him in ways that he still struggled with. Dante had never admitted it to anyone, but he had once stolen a bottle of his grandmother's pills in hopes of escaping the pain. Unfortunately, or fortunately, he had taken a massive dose of laxatives. His grandmother had always assumed that one of the kids at school who teased him had played some practical joke that got out of hand.

Dante had never disabused her of that assumption. "If you don't want to talk about your fathers, that's fine," he added.

"I am happy to speak of my fathers. I had a far better relationship with them than with my mother." Regi detoured around a huge stump with a jagged top that smelled of wood rot. "Fathers' years are when a young Kowri goes to work with a parent of his choice. Most Kowri choose to attend the workplace of one of their fathers because leaving your mother's side is seen as a rite of passage. Fathers' years are the first chance a Kowri has to make educational choices and to start exploring the world outside of the mother's sphere of influence."

"But Kowri could stay with their mothers during their father years?" If so, that seemed like an inaccurate name.

"They could if they wished to, but most take at least a year or two to explore other careers. I sought to leave my mother as soon as I could. I often found myself relegated to a corner while she tended a difficult pregnancy, so I chose to go with my da-father the day I began my second set of years."

Dante was starting to get a picture of neglect and emotional abuse from Regi's stories. Maybe that was wrong—maybe he was projecting his own abandonment issues onto Regi's life—but if he ever met Regi's mother, he had a few things to say to that woman. No one should care more about their goddess than their five-year-old child. "What was your father like?"

"Pertin a'Qis," Regi said in a fond voice.

"Pertin." Dante rolled the unfamiliar syllables around in his mouth. "Is Qis his goddess?"

"Qis is the god of old-growth forests and secrets." Regi paused and looked about. The trees had started to thin enough that sunlight made a patchwork quilt out of the ground; however, huge trees still dominated the land. "He watches places like this. I spent my first year sanding pieces of wood in Pertin's shop. He is a carver and very respected for his ability to find the shapes inside the wood."

"I guess I hadn't thought of an advanced space-race appreciating wood carving. My grandfather had a shop set up in a shed behind their house. I used to hear his saw running in the morning when I stayed with them over summer. He died not long after I started school."

"I am sorry."

Dante shrugged. "So what was life like working with Pertin?"

"He found beauty in every piece of wood. When I went to work with him, he had this huge project—a totem of the growing season sacred animals carved from one piece of wood larger than Alb's house. It was so impressive." Regi stopped walking, and for a second, he stared into space. Then he shook his head and gave Dante a crooked smile before he took lead again. "I always thought it was unfair that over and over again he would have to abandon his projects because my mother would get some goddess-inspired urge to travel."

"Your gods make life difficult."

"That is true." Regi was silent for a time. The only sound was the crunch of leaves under their feet as they walked. Eventually he said, "Life was far easier for my di-father, Rel a'Mufvu. His work involves programming, and he specializes in personal networks and small-scale communications systems. If he had a computer, he could do his work from anywhere."

"That would make travel easier," Dante agreed.

"I worked with Pertin first, but I spent most of my fathers' years with Rel. He taught me about computer searches and network logic." Regi grimaced. "I had once thought to train to better understand the Gavd ships I planned to serve on, but the universe rarely listens to the plans a child makes for his own future. Luckily, it turns out that computer logic transfers from one culture to another. When I went to the Academy to serve in the Coalition's military, my years with Rel helped me understand the nuance of computer networks from a Coalition standpoint."

Dante did a bit of mental math and figured that Regi must've been seven or eight when he was working on computer programming. It did seem a little backwards to teach a kid advanced programming when reading and writing weren't fully developed, but given how schools worked on Earth, Dante was loath to criticize anyone else. Texas had decided that privatizing as many of the government functions as possible was the best way to avoid Supreme Court decisions that had given legal rights to an ever-expanding group of citizens. Texas had become a strange patchwork of private and parochial schools, all using government vouchers to take public money into the private realm where discrimination could thrive. Compared to Earth, Regi's people sounded downright sane. Mostly. Siger did sour Dante on the Kowri a bit.

"What if a child doesn't like any of the careers of his parents? Trust me, I had no interest in anything my father did. And even if I wanted to grow up and be a lawyer—which I didn't—my father's law firm was no place for a child. He worked criminal cases as a prosecutor, and kids don't need to hear those sorts of details." Dante shivered in horror at the thought.

"Children are often shown a limited scope of a parent's work. However, if a child shows proficiency in an area outside the parents' areas of expertise, family members will offer to take the child during their fathers' years."

"So it's an early-outreach internship rather than years that belong solely to the fathers."

"Very little of that translated, but from the tone and limited understanding I have of your words, I would agree," Regi said.

Silence gathered between them, and Dante was slapping away some insects when he asked, "What if a parent is a horrible influence? What if a parent puts their kids in a position where they're exposed to dangerous equipment or they're asked to do dangerous work?"

Regi's ears dipped. "I will not lie. It does happen. Gavd ships must investigate accusations of that sort more often than is appropriate for a species that claims to serve the gods. When such happens, a child might be given to someone else to supervise for their fathers' years or they may be moved to another family." Regi hesitated, and Dante nearly walked into his back because he was distracted by a swarm of gnats or gnat-like flying pests. Dante put his hands on Regi's shoulders to prevent a collision.

Regi turned to study him. "I try to avoid difficult discussions of my people's shortcomings with others from the Coalition." Given that the other crew members had a negative view of Kowri, Dante could understand that.

"I don't plan on telling them anything. Hell, Ter seems to think he knows everything already, so what's the point of even trying to talk to him?" Dante grinned at Regi.

Regi brayed a laugh. The explosive sound resembled a donkey's alarm call more than laughter, but Dante was growing use to it. "I should tell Ter that you said as much." He started walking again.

"He doesn't listen to you either, so he'll probably nod while you talk, and the whole time he'll be focusing on his computer. So, feel free."

"You show great insight, especially given that the translator has such limited function when it comes to your language."

Dante shrugged even though Regi couldn't see the gesture with his back turned. "Because I didn't know the words, I started looking at people's body language the way I would watch a skittish horse. People communicate a lot of what they're thinking through their bodies."

Regi glanced over his shoulder, studying Dante before saying, "I had never considered applying the skills of an animal tender to sapient species. You are an impressive person, Dante a'Texas."

"Now don't go telling people that. I don't want to have to live up to their expectations."

"One of the most dangerous goddesses of the universe watches you. I promise you that she expects you to live up to her expectations."

Dante winced. "That does not make me feel better."

"As I said, you are a wise man. Children dream of being exalted, but adult Kowri understand that when the gods provide the twin blessings, they always provide more of the first than the second."

Dante understood that. And it seemed like Regi was right that they were far more interested in creating chaos and inspiring disasters than in opening opportunities. "Have you considered telling them to knock it off?"

"And who would tell a god that she had to change how she interacted with her subjects?"

"I would." Dante looked up at the thinning canopy of leaves overhead. "Divashi, you gotta stop shoving us face first into problems."

Regi's ears went all the way back and he spun around to consider Dante with wide eyes.

"What?" Dante asked with exaggerated innocence.

"You are a menace," Regi said.

Dante grinned. "You say the sweetest things." Dante was about to launch into an irreverent condemnation of Divashi's habit of meddling like the bored church ladies who had retired and had nothing better to do than pry into everyone else's business, but a chunk of tree next to Dante's head exploded into splinters. Dante stared at the giant wound opened into the tree's trunk for the half second it took Regi to tackle him to the ground.

"Incoming weapons fire!" Regi called out as though he had a platoon of soldiers ready to return fire. Unfortunately, their only back up was trees. Another loud pop preceded a lower branch crashing down near them.

Regi pulled Dante behind the arched roots of the closest tree. "What the hell is that?" Dante demanded. He was hoping Regi would come up with some bizarre alien explanation like ball lightning.

"That the hell is someone trying to kill us," Regi said solemnly. Well, shit.

Chapter Fourteen

"Where is that coming from?" Dante asked.

Regi was draped over Dante's back, keeping him pressed to the ground. "There's at least one shooter in the east. Possibly two." Probably two because Regi had heard two different discharge whines. Most Kowri favored one hand over the other for precision work such as shooting, so two weapons implied two shooters. "We need to move before they have a chance to get closer."

"Thank God for bad aim," Dante said. He wiped the side of his face where white leaf slime stained his cheek. "Either that or thank Divashi for ruining the shooter's aim."

"Thank the universal powers later. We need to move before they close the distance between us." Regi slid off Dante's back and kept low as he retreated behind the nearest ifah tree. They were large enough to absorb the energy blasts, or at least Regi hoped they were. He had left Empire space without ever having trained on Empire weapons. He couldn't assume they had the same limitations of Coalition weaponry.

Dante followed without comment even though his height made it more difficult for him to stay within the limited cover. Regi suspected their attackers were using the rise to the south to hide, so when he reached low ground, he started to run. With every step, he feared the burn of energy searing his skin, but the pain failed to materialize. Not even the whine of a weapon discharge marked his retreat.

Dante ran after him, bent at the waist in a manner that appeared uncomfortable. "Are you crazy?" he demanded.

"I don't have any brain dysfunction I know of, although my mother would likely disagree," Regi answered. Dante stared at him, his mouth open. After waiting two or three seconds for a response, Regi dismissed any concerns Dante might have for his brain's health and ran for deeper woods. An unknown number of pursuers wished to kill them, and they could not waste time.

Regi stopped in the shadow of the largest ifah tree he'd ever seen. Dante slid to a stop beside him, skidding in the damp leaves so the scent of sweet rot swirled around them. "They could have shot you in the back!" Dante said loudly before targeting Regi's arm for a strike that was so impotent Regi feared for Dante's ability to defend himself. While Dante had acted in a way that was both efficient and effective in their battle against the Styl pirate, the weak nature of the strike made Regi doubt Dante's ability to protect himself in such rough territory.

"The angle of the fire suggested they are using the rise. I was not in sight from that rise when I chose to run."

"That's a lot of faith to put into an assumption, especially when someone is shooting at you." Dante's voice suggested anger.

"I am a trained security officer. Judging angles of fire and taking reasonable risks are part of my training."

"Still risky," Dante muttered.

Despite the danger, Regi glanced in his direction. "Are you worried about me?"

"I do like you despite your recklessness with your own life."

"Reckless would be standing still and allowing them to gain ground on us. We must get out of this area." He turned his attention back to the woods before running for a rise that could provide more cover. A thicket of berry brambles provided only visual cover; the vegetation would not stop even the weakest of weapons. Their main problem lay in the fact that Regi had no idea how to reach the assistance Alb had sent them. He could call her again and request a new rendezvous, but others must have tracked his communicator. He was loath to turn it on again and help their enemies pinpoint their location.

Regi ran until his breath was coming in heavy gasps. He worried the level of physical exertion would overtax Dante's system, but Dante had not only kept up, but he struggled less than Regi. Given that Dante was a fragile species, that was a stiff condemnation of Regi's fitness regime.

Dante waited until they had reached the shadow of a boulder before he asked, "Where are we going now?" He had begun breathing out of his mouth. Even after seeing him change his method of breathing several times, it was still odd.

"I am unsure. Our enemy waits in the travelway to the temple, but I am unsure how we can get around them to reach the assistance Alb has promised us."

Dante winced. "Are you entirely sure that Alb is on our side?"

A bone-deep shock rattled Regi to his core. "Were she not ethical, she would not be an exalted. If she is against us, that is as good as suggesting that the gods are against us. The gods have never turned Kowri against Kowri." If they ever did, Regi was unsure how his people would survive.

"Maybe Alb's god is the one trying to stab us in the back. I've never had good luck with people who like to write down other's stories." Dante muttered the last bit under his breath.

Regi shook his head. "The gods are united in their course. Any debates they may have with each other do not spill over into their handling of our world."

Dante grimaced before his expression cleared, and he gave a single nod. "You know your gods better than I do, so I will take your word. So, if we need to find the Gavd folks trying to rescue us, how do we get past the guys with the guns?"

"That is an excellent question."

"That is why I asked it."

"Unfortunately, I lack an equally excellent answer," Regi confessed. "Any attempt to circumnavigate our adversaries would require us to move closer to them at some point."

"And you don't have a weapon?"

Regi's hand fell to his anelace. "Not one that can counter their energy weapons."

"I was hoping that you had smuggled an illegal weapon in your back pocket."

"I am unsure what pocket is, but I assure you that I would not smuggle a weapon on a Kowri world. Kowri have technology that enables them to identify those who illegally possess weaponry, and I would prefer not to aggravate a leadership which is currently debating whether to eject or execute crew members whose safety I am responsible for."

A frown flickered across Dante's face before he said, "You bring up a valid concern."

"It is certainly valid from my point of view." Regi lived with the constant terror that his decision to request asylum inside Kowri space would lead to the deaths of the crew he was not only duty-bound to protect but that he liked. "We must continue moving. If they are hunting us, they likely have technology which allows them to track our location." Regi set a brisk pace back towards the deeper woods.

"This is not a fair fight," Dante complained. The words were soft and spoken with an excess of air.

"I rarely expect criminals to concern themselves with fairness. In fact, I find they usually eschew any sense of fairness in their dealings."

"I'll take your word for it. On my planet, it's generally the leaders who eschew fairness." Dante blew out a heavy breath. "I need to apologize to my English teacher because I insisted I would never need the words she made me memorize for Friday tests."

Regi didn't want to exhaust himself or Dante, so he slowed to a fair trot that would hopefully keep the enemy behind them while still allowing them to watch their footing.

Dante kept pace. "If those guys have pebafri, there is no way we can outrun them, and I get the feeling those horns are not for decoration."

"They are not, but no criminals would dare bring those beasts into the woods." The thought of their pursuers even trying was laughable. Regi could remember the plots of many children's stories where such foolishness led to the gods raining havoc down on the heads of the fools who had tempted fate in such a way.

"Why not? Both of us rode a pebafri into these woods."

"The animals are sacred to Gavd, and riding one is an invitation for Gavd to involve himself in one's business. Criminals avoid sacred animals so that they may avoid the attention of any god who may foil their plans." Regi divided his attention between the ground directly in front of him where any potential trip hazards lay in wait and the contour of the land behind. If the enemy could reach the crest before Regi and Dante found new cover, they would be exposed because the trees were not yet dense enough to offer adequate protection.

However, Dante grabbed his arm with surprising force. "Wait," Dante said. "Pebafri will go the temple, won't they?"

Regi glanced toward the ridge and considered dragging Dante to a safer position, but that appeared rude. "At least some wild pebafri in their area likely will as they follow god-touched members of the herd."

"Is that pebafri headed to the temple?" Dante pointed north where an ancient male with a gray muzzle picked his way over a bramble of dead branches.

"Perhaps. It is difficult to know which animals have been touched by a god and which have not."

"Yes, but we have the advantage that we have been touched by a god, so the sacred animals won't kill us, correct?"

"I assume so." Any Kowri who heard such a statement from Regi would charge him with sacrilege for including an outsider in that assumption, but Regi did assume that Divashi lavished at least as much attention on Dante as any other exalted who answered to the Lady of poisons. And Regi was not alone in that assumption.

"But I'm guessing that anyone who is trying to commit murder is on the gods' naughty list." Dante sounded oddly gleeful about that proclamation.

"The concept of a naughty list is unusual, but in general I believe I would agree." Regi had no idea why Dante wanted such irrelevant pieces of information.

An uneven grin spread across Dante's face. "If these pebafri are god-touched, do you think they will let us near?"

A second male appeared next to the first. This one was not as large, but it had the darker colors of a younger individual. "If they are not god-touched, they will either evade or eviscerate us. What are you suggesting?"

"I'm suggesting that we use your people's prejudices against them. They don't want to ride a pebafri because it would be bad luck and attract the attention of the gods, so do you think they would be willing to kill one?"

Horror washed through Regi at the very thought. He had been forced to kill a pebafri once because a predator had grievously wounded it, and even knowing that he was serving Gavd by sparing his sacred animal the pain of a slow and torturous death, killing it had been one of the most difficult moments in Regi's life.

"I can tell by looking at your face that killing a pebafri is anathema to you. And that means they will avoid it. We can follow the pebafri to the back door of the temple and call Alb from there."

The plan was both simple and audacious. However, Regi could imagine an impossible number of ways it could go wrong. "If they have proper scanners, they will still be able to position themselves in such a way as to shoot us without injuring the animals." Regi feared their pursuers could have any number of Kowri weapons that would make tracking them too easy, and Regi's understanding of his people's security measures was inadequate. He knew more about Styl weaponry than Kowri.

"Unless your people are far better with firearms than mine, placing a shot between moving animals is not easy."

Regi tugged on his ear and considered trajectories. Dante was right about that. If there were even two or three animals between them and the shooters, getting a shot would become exponentially more difficult. Other forms began to move through the shadows. A female with two spindly legged children appeared, a clump of vegetation hanging from her mouth. Another wide with pregnancy appeared and then two more males—young ones who leapt over brambles with such enthusiasm that Kowri could have stood beneath their leap and no hoof would have touched a hair.

Regi closed his eyes and touched his knuckles to his temples as he tried to decide whether this was a god sign or a terrible idea which appeared plausible only because he could not come up with another. In stories, exalteds always recognized the hands of the gods in their lives. Reality was more ambiguous. And as much is Regi knew his gods and loved them, he did not want to put their safety in enormous hands that might prove too large for the lives of two small beings. "What you are suggesting is a grave risk. You assume the enemy will not target us within the herd or follow us long enough to kill us as we attempt to leave the herd on the edge of town."

"I assume that murderers like to function in the shadows."

Regi sucked air through his teeth. Dante did have a point. Before he could marshal another argument, Dante strode toward the pebafri herd with a confidence that made it clear he had been the huuman equivalent of Siger. More than a dozen pebafri now wandered through the dappled shadow formed by swaying branches overhead. These were wild pebafri with mottled coats designed far more for camouflage than to impress a potential buyer. Dante reached the closest—one of the young males—and rested a hand on the animal's flank. The pebafri swung his head around, juvenile horns still dangerous even if they were half the size of the adult ones. However, the creature only sniffed Dante before nipping at his pebafri playmate. The second male came over and stood on Dante's other side.

Dante smiled. His small form was dwarfed by even the young pebafri, so hope started to grow in Regi's heart. He walked over, and the pebafri shifted to allow him to stand next to Dante.

Regi caught Dante's oddly shaped hand in his. "If my enemies manage to outmaneuver the gods, I would wish for you to take whatever cover is possible. If cornered, I will give you as much time as I can to escape." Regi squeezed Dante's hand. Dante had been watching the pebafri with wonder and some emotion that reminded Regi of parental love, but now he turned to Regi. He captured Regi's free hand in his so that now they stood with both hands joining them.

"If you're going down, I'm going down. But my preference would be for us to survive long enough to make those bastards sorry that they hunted us. So don't you dare talk about losing this fight."

"I am attempting to be practical." Regi loathed considering any alternatives that did not include his own survival, but it was his obligation to be practical and to ensure the survival of as many people as possible. "These people are offended by my status as exalted and my work advocating for Divashi's positions. If this plan fails and we divide their attention, they will focus on me. That will give you a greater probability of surviving to reach town." The logic of the argument was unassailable. These enemies might hate outsiders, but they would not feel threatened by them. Regi, on the other hand, posed a threat.

Dante shook his head. "If I wanted to live by probabilities, I would have killed myself long before I met you. How improbable was it that you found me on that ship?"

"The gods' twin blessings led me there, but wise Kowri say that those who depend on either of the gods' blessings deserve neither and will prove themselves fools."

"I get that, but I'm not leaving you no matter what happens. There are few enough people in my life that I genuinely like that I am unwilling to give up on one."

"That's foolish."

"Then I'm a fool, and if you want to keep me from getting shot, you need to keep yourself out of the line of fire."

"I don't want you to die, even if the gods decide it's my time."

Dante smiled. "I think you're saying you like me, too."

"Of course I like you. You are challenging and confusing and you accept the Kowri parts of me in ways that Coalition members never have and accept the Coalition parts of me in ways that Kowri never will. But that is why I am telling you that if the enemy finds us, allow them to target me. I would rather give you a chance to continue being brave and challenging and odd. I don't want to die knowing that you are fated to die next to me."

Dante blew out an explosive breath. "After we both survive this, I'm sending you for therapy and possibly antidepressants."

The translator offered a strange amalgam of ideas with the last word, but the general idea was clear. "I admire your loyalty and optimism, but I would feel better if I had your promise that you will put yourself first."

"Tough, because I won't give you that promise. Now move your ass because these pebafri are moving."

The animals started moving with more purpose toward the ridge where the enemy waited. And Dante moved with them. Realizing that he had lost any chance to debate, Regi slipped between the pregnant female and the oldest male. This was a horrible plan but given that they were unarmed with an unknown number of enemies hunting them, faith in the gods was the only advantage they had. Regi never expected an outsider to make that argument for him, but then again, in all the time he had served in the Coalition, he had never met another outsider like Dante.

Chapter Fifteen

"Stop making a target of your head." Regi caught the back of Dante's shirt and pulled his head down below the level of the pebafri's withers.

Dante bent lower and grimaced. "Never before has my height been such a disadvantage."

Regi watched for a moment to make sure Dante remained within the old pebafri's shadow before he moved his gaze to the line of trees to their north. Siger and one other attacker had already shown themselves on that distant horizon, something which frightened Regi far more than the occasional burst of weapons fire. While the energy blasts had never come close to either of them, Siger and his compatriots had allowed themselves to be seen, which suggested that the two men still felt they had the upper hand.

Had they shown concern about preserving the illusion of their innocence, they would have fled. After all, the cold-weather temple was so close that Regi could see the wide, arched doorway through which the sacred animals entered the temple proper. If Regi called for assistance from Gavd followers now, that assistance could arrive in mere minutes. Even walking, Regi and Dante would reach the temple within an hour.

"What's wrong?" Dante crouched beside the old pebafri that plodded toward the temple. When they had first left the cover of trees, Dante had been more fluid in his movements even if the practicalities of cover required him to walk hunched. But now, his movements took on a jerky quality and he leaned against the pebafri, his odd-fingered hand smearing the dust on the pebafri's coat. Regi suspected Dante was in pain, but he refrained from complaining. Regi grieved that he could not spare Dante this physical discomfort, but more than that, he wished he could escape the sinking feeling that he was leading an innocent man into a trap designed for Regi.

Dante stumbled, and in his recovery, he stood straight for a moment, and either Siger or his compatriot opened fire before Regi could react. Dante doubled over so quickly that Regi feared he had suffered an injury, but Dante chuckled. "Someone needs to spend more time at the firing range, thank God."

"I assume a range is a place of practice, and I am more than happy to say they need no more practice. They need someone to remove any access to weapons," Regi countered. He wondered if their enemies hoped to kill Dante as well, or if they only hoped that Regi would expose his position to cover Dante were the other man to be injured. Even knowing that was likely Siger's plan, Regi would abandon the cover offered by this slow-moving herd to protect Dante to the best of his ability. He could do nothing less for an individual who showed such exquisite loyalty.

"We should be to the temple within the hour," Regi said with a reassuring smile.

Dante's eyebrows became off-balanced. "Then why do you look so worried?"

Regi carefully schooled his expression into one of neutrality. "Interpreting facial gestures is difficult when two individuals do not share the same cultural background. Even individuals from one world will sometimes struggle to correctly interpret non-verbal communication from another who comes from a geographically isolated area."

Dante blew air out of his mouth. "That sounds like a fancy way of saying that you don't want to admit why you're concerned."

Sometimes Regi wished that Dante was less insightful. "There is armed enemy seeking to shoot us. Is that not a reason for concern?" A freio lumbered past the herd. Most Kowri would shake in fear at being near such a creature, but Dante didn't spare it much more than a glance. Either he did not recognize the prodigious danger or he trusted the gods to keep their sacred animals in hand. The creature would not have left its mountainous home had not the Lord of retribution called him.

"Given they don't seem to be able to hit the broadside of a barn, it really isn't," Dante said quickly. While Regi was unclear on the meaning of "*barn*", he understood the general message. Most Kowri didn't train on weapons, so he hadn't expected proficiency, but this level of ineptitude did make him wonder if the gods were intervening.

"We will be fine." Regi hoped that by saying as much, he could shape reality with his words. Before Kowri reached the stars they had believed that possible.

"We're better off than the other guys. The pebafri are about as mean as a polecat."

"Are polecats mean?"

"Ferrets?" Dante grinned widely. "They are mean enough to eat a man's leg."

They were ferocious predators then. Regi had to admit that he had not expected the two young pebafri to be quite so violent, but when four enemies had attempted to leave the cover of the trees and take a more direct approach to killing Regi and Dante, their juvenile antics had become a vicious attack that had left two of the attackers on the ground. Since then, Siger and his remaining compatriot had followed from a distance as they kept to the trees. The pebafri had stalked the edge of the woods for a while. It was as if Gavd himself guided their fury. Regi knew that that was an overly optimistic estimate of the god's ability since he had larger issues to watch, but right now Regi wanted to cling to the childlike hope that the gods would save them.

Considering that Siger still had the confidence to follow, Regi needed the assistance of the gods. He hoped his story did not end with the gods being distracted or blinded to the events on the mortal plane while he bled to death. Too many stories ended that way.

"Regi, I have a problem with being denied information. Something has you worried, and I don't think it's Siger's terrible aim."

For a moment, Regi considered bluffing. If he were out here with one of his Coalition underlings on their first shipboard mission, he would have. However, he owed Dante more. And selfishly, he wanted someone else to bear this burden with him. "Reasonable creatures would have fled before coming so close to the temple and the considerable resources Gavd's followers dedicate to enforcing laws." A female pebafri detoured around a thorn bush, shoving Regi out of her path. Dante caught him with a hand under Regi's elbow. They stood still for a moment, the herd slowly wandering past them. But then Dante cleared this throat and trotted to catch up with the large male he preferred to use for cover.

"Are you suggesting that Siger and his idiot friend don't know how to secure their own best interest, or are you suggesting that there is some trap that we are walking into?"

Regi was, once again, impressed with the insight Dante showed into the situation. Perhaps he had been training young ones straight out of Coalition academies too long because he considered such common sense rare. "I hate to rely on the patience of the gods to prevent any possible trap. The gods are not interested in the survival of individual Kowri or outsiders as much as ensuring they guide the species down the correct path. Our lives are insignificant compared to that."

"Divashi considers us significant."

Regi wished he could trust that. "She wished to bring her dops home, and we were a necessary part of that."

"Do you believe that your gods care about pebafri and dops more than us?"

"They are sacred animals," Regi explained. "And even then, their lives are sometimes used to advance a goal. Either Gavd or Divashi chose to send those two young pebafri after the attackers. They could have died, but the gods pursue their own ends and will risk individual lives to achieve it."

"So, you're saying the animals are exactly as sacred as we are."

Regi blinked. He was exalted and he had grown up around exalteds, but he had never considered those Kowri sacred to their gods. He had never considered himself sacred. Sometimes Dante made him see the world in uncomfortable ways. "Perhaps," he admitted, "but we cannot rely on them to preserve our flesh. We approach the temple, and those two still do not retreat."

Dante glanced in the direction of their followers. "Should we call for help?"

"That is the logical course," Regi said, "which is why I hesitate to take it. Unpredictability is a strategic advantage."

"Your people are kinda set in your ways. I love horses and I'm starting to think kindly about pebafri, but if one attacked me, I would shoot it. But you predicted that these guys wouldn't take the risk of attracting Gavd's attention, and you're right."

Regi winced when his boot sank into a soft spot formed by an excess of animal excrement that had gathered in a shallow hole. He stomped to remove the excess material and considered Dante's words. His people were predictable. And he was leading them toward the temple. Going to the temple was predictable. "I could call Alb," Regi said. So far, he had not reached out to her. Dante's words were like gibuks crawling through his brain, poisoning his thoughts.

"Do you think we should?" Dante asked, his voice devoid of emotion.

"The gods are united in supporting the greater good of the Kowri people. If Divashi and Gavd guide us, then the Lady of stories is also our ally." And that meant Alb would assist them. The logic was unassailable.

"Then call her," Dante said. His voice was so without inflection that Regi knew he still suspected Alb of giving away their location. Given that Siger could just as easily have tracked the communicator once Regi reconnected to the network, suspecting her seemed unreasonable. And yet...

The silence continued as they plodded. So many large animals walked this ground that it was as hard-packed and devoid of life as any tiled over city surface on a Coalition world. Regi couldn't delay for long because every step brought them closer to the temple. Overhead, birds soared, dropping into the hypaethoros from above, and a variety of poisonous creatures wandered to and from, their paths taking them outside the pebafri herd where Regi and Dante had taken shelter.

Regi waited until the entrance loomed near before he reached for his communicator. Soon they would have to leave the shelter of the herd and move around to the front of the temple, and that would be the moment of greatest danger.

He spoke clearly despite the fear souring his stomach. "I am Regi a'Divashi. Connect me to Alb a'Oba and any senior follower of Gavd currently assigned to preventing or investigating crime." The communicator offered several tones as various individuals connected, but Regi waited until he saw Alb's name listed as receiving before he spoke. "Dante and I are within sight of the rear entrance to the cold weather temple. Siger a'Gavd and at least one of his associates have shot at us multiple times, and we have taken refuge inside a pebafri herd moving toward the temple. Once Dante and I separate from the animals, I fear Siger or others will shoot at us again."

"What is the origin of the conflict?" an unfamiliar female asked.

"He believes Gavd is the true god and those who follow Divashi and the Lady herself are a corruption." That was answered with a profound silence. No one took more offense at Gavd monotheists than Gavd followers.

"How close are you to the temple?" Alb asked. "I am moving toward you, although age means I move more slowly than I once did."

"Ten minutes walking would have us at the arch," Regi said. The pebafri began to walk faster now, but Alb spoke before Regi could amend his answer.

"Stay to the right, and I will meet you near the last house on the temple side," Alb said. That would likely be Nawr a'Ectipic's house. The exalteds were often the only ones who wanted houses bordering the cold-weather travel path. Other Kowri found it discomforting to find a freio outside their window, even a sacred one.

"We shall send enforcers," the female follower of Gavd said. Tones sounded as the various listeners disconnected, including Alb.

Regi put his communicator into his pocket and eyed the two sides of the temple. "If we wish to be unpredictable, we should move to the left." Regi felt like a boy trying to cheat on a temple test requiring him to identify hundreds of gods. Betraying Alb was that difficult. Denying any exalted was that difficult, even when one was exalted.

"That would work," Dante said, his tone still neutral. "That means we have to get by that creature." Dante nodded toward the freio.

"I worry less about a sacred animal than I do about the chance that Siger or the others might encounter a miracle and fire a weapon in a way that proves dangerous."

"That is a point." Dante huffed. "So, left it is. Is it me, or are the pebafri moving faster?"

"They know there is food ahead of them," Regi said.

"That explains it. Every horse I've ever ridden wants to get the bit in its teeth once it sees the barn." Dante shifted pace to one that included far more bouncing in addition to more speed. The gait worried Regi since each upward movement put the back of Dante's head in danger, but they had to keep up with the herd. Regi lengthened his own stride and tucked his arms close. They halved the remaining distance before a familiar burst of weapons' fire interrupted the rhythm created by the pebafri's hooves.

The large, old male screamed, a huge burn appearing high on his withers and up onto his neck. He bared his teeth at the sky and started to run.

"Oh fuck," Dante said. Regi didn't even have time to worry about the poorly timed reference to copulation because all the pebafri began to run. Dante took off at a sprint that would be impressive even for a Kowri, and Regi raced after him. The pebafri were panicked, and two more blasts from a weapon did not improve the situation. To keep some cover, Regi poured every ounce of energy into staying within the shelter of the herd—a herd that was moving to the right. Dante moved with them, and Regi followed. If this was a trap, Dante was set to spring it, and Regi did not have the air to argue the wisdom of that action.

The scream of frim filled the air as a flock burst out of the top of the temple, their raucous cries even louder than the pounding of pebafri hooves. The freio bellowed a challenge before heat seared the side of Regi's face. The near miss of an energy weapon left his skin tingling and hot. They were to the far right of the gate now and Regi forced his aching muscles to carry him faster—to get to Dante's side before their enemies could close in on them.

Alb came out from behind a house, a dozen individuals near her. Regi had a moment of relief before his brain noted the da-males at her side raise their weapon.

Chapter Sixteen

Dante was sprinting for the safety of the townhouses that lined the side of the temple one moment, and the next a strong arm caught him around the waist and flung him into the air at such an odd angle that his arms flailed, and Peaches offered an angry chittering that could only be dop profanity.

Hitting the ground hard, Dante cupped his hands around Peaches to prevent her from either getting flung wide or crushed as he rolled. Before he could gather his wits well enough to ask Regi for an explanation, the shimmering heat of an alien laser gun seared the air above their heads. The guards Dante had been rushing toward pointed weapons in their direction. Regi plastered himself to Dante's back, pressing Dante to the hard-packed ground as weapons fired.

Shit.

Dante usually liked to be in the right. He reveled in it. After a childhood of being told in unambiguous terms that his very existence was wrong, he found any opportunity to crow about his successes. However, he was not as sanguine about finding out that Alb was the enemy. Dante looked to Regi for strategy. Right now, panicking animals gave them some cover, but that wouldn't last long. "Run for the freio." Regi gestured towards the enormous lumbering beast, a cross between a bear and a saber-tooth tiger.

Dante had been trying very hard to ignore the beast and deny the bone-deep terror at being near it. Being told to run towards it was a step too far. Panic blossomed in Dante's chest. "What?" he yelped.

Before Regi could answer, more energy weapons discharged, super-heating the air around them. Given a choice between being shot or being mauled by a saber-tooth tiger-bear, Dante would rather be shot. However, Regi thought the big fucking predator was the better option. Great. Wonderful.

"Go, go, go," Regi ordered. He rolled off Dante's back. Dante held Peaches close and sprinted towards the predator. In horror movies, every time someone looked behind them, they tripped and fell, and Dante did not want to be a stereotype of a stupid human. So he kept his eyes on the lumbering beast as he weaved between the other animals, some of whom raced for the temple, and some of whom fled it.

Unlike the other animals, the saber-tooth bear seemed unconcerned with the drama. It neither flinched nor wavered as it trundled towards the temple. When one of the energy weapons discharged close enough to make the air around the animal shimmer, it stopped and glanced in the direction of their attackers with disdain, which made Dante suspect that anyone who managed to hit the beast would regret it for the remainder of their brutally short lives. A few feet from the bear-thing, Dante stumbled and caught himself with a hand against the furred hide. Like the Kowri themselves, the beast was striped, but it had dark brown and vivid red stripes that reminded Dante of poisonous snake colors.

Dante searched for Regi, assuming that he couldn't be more than a few steps behind. He was wrong.

Regi had taken Dante's position beside the huge, old stallion. The creature was injured and struggling, but, like the rest of the pebafri, he was still moving towards Alb and her men. That meant Regi was moving that way as well.

"Oh fuck, no," Dante whispered in horror. He tried to move toward Regi and whatever suicidal attack plan the idiot had formed. Unfortunately, the saber-tooth bear's enormous head swung around. Dante was so out of breath and had such a stitch in his side that he had to grab the animal's fur to keep from falling. However, he had their most effective weapon—Peaches. Dante needed to reach Regi.

When Dante tried to move around the saber-tooth bear again, the beast blocked. Since predators didn't act like this, Dante assumed a Kowri god was riding the animal. "He needs help, and either I'm going to help Regi, or you are. But I will not let him throw his life away on your agenda. His life is not expendable." Regi had seen up close the nasty burn the old stallion had taken, the weeping edges of the wound and the charred bits of flesh. As bad as that had been, Dante didn't want to consider Regi dying with those same horrific marks.

"Get out of my way." Dante tried and failed to go around the beast again. Dante couldn't see over the creature's back, and it had moved to block Dante's view, so Dante crouched to look under the creature's belly.

"Regi!" he screamed. The air was raucous with the calls of animals and the pounding of hooves hitting the hard ground, and Regi didn't react. "Regi!" Dante screamed so loud that his throat hurt. Regi continued his lone charge using the inadequate cover offered by the stumbling stallion. Several of Alb's henchmen were on the ground, and Dante was unsure of the reason until the two halfgrown pebafri raced through the ranks of gunmen.

The goons turned their guns on the animals, but the youngsters darted and swerved with the nimbleness of yearlings. Their antics appeared playful until one leapt over the gunman's head, and hoof met with skull. The gunman collapsed. Another fired a shot that caught the pebafri across the rump. The yearling screamed in pain and both young pebafri raced away, bucking as though trying to rid themselves of unwanted riders.

Weapon fire came fast now, and several gunmen focused on the slowing stallion. The animal stumbled to his knees, and Regi was left dangerously exposed. Regi had said that the gods provided only opportunity and any Kowri who relied on them would die because their hands were too large to shelter a creature as small as a Kowri. Dante marched up to the saber-tooth bear's head and stared it straight in the eye.

"You get your oversized hands down here, and you protect him, or I swear to God I will burn your fucking temple to the ground. I will raze it. I will have Ter teach me engines so I can overload one and blow your temple to smithereens. I will salt the ground so that nothing ever grows again if you don't protect him."

The saber-tooth bear snorted hot air that smelled of leaf rot.

Peaches chattered at him desperately, her paws tangled in his hair as she sat on his shoulder.

Half afraid to look, Dante watched under the beast's belly. The stallion had fallen, one leg still kicking in the air to suggest the creature was alive and suffering. But against all odds, Regi was alive. He was grappling with one of the gunmen, each holding one side of an alien laser gun as they wrestled.

A second gunmen ran toward the fray. Dante pointed at the new gunmen. "Get him. Stop him. Eat him. I don't care but do something." When nothing happened, Dante grabbed the saber-tooth bear's beard and pulled its head around and pointed at the running henchman. "Stop him," Dante demanded. The saber-tooth bear snorted again, his leaf-rot breath enough to make Dante nauseated. But screams came from the air.

Miniature feathered pterodactyls screamed down the sky. Five or six of them swooped toward the approaching reinforcements, making the man take off running the other way. At the very least, that took him out of the conflict, but Dante hoped the damn birds ate the asshole's liver.

Regi still wrestled with the gunman, but both were on the ground now. If Kowri lives were as small as Regi insisted, their gods would be unable to separate the combatants. That meant it was Dante's turn. He started to go around the saber-tooth bear, but the stubborn thing stepped in his way again. "I'm going to help him." Dante shoved the beast. He got another rotten leaf whoosh of air across his face. Peaches chattered so it was difficult for Dante to even hear his own voice, but Dante didn't back down to slavers, and he wouldn't for alien gods, either. He addressed the bear since he didn't want to curse out Peaches. Maybe she was just as connected to the gods as this damned bear, but Dante liked her.

"I don't worship you guys." He poked the saber-tooth bear's shoulder. "In fact, I think you're assholes. You damn near killed Regi and his entire crew because you wanted your dops saved. Even now, you're letting your people debate whether to kill a crew of good people who helped. So, you don't have a whole lot of credit with me. So don't you fucking get in my way because the offer to burn your fucking temple down is still fucking on the table."

The saber-tooth bear was unimpressed.

"You!" Across the near-empty field, Alb pointed at him. She was so old that her stripes were gray, but when she ran, her steps were sure. Worse, she lifted a shortened version of an alien ray gun.

Caught between backing up Regi and fleeing, Dante froze, unable to do either. "I should probably run, huh?" Dante asked the saber-tooth bear. It blinked at him while Peaches chitter-screamed in his ear. The far side of the temple was too far to run with a stitch in his side, so Dante dashed for the arched entry to the temple's sacred garden. He would apologize to any offended Kowri later; right now he wanted to find cover.

The moment he passed the arched entry, the humidity increased as water trickled over the stone walls on either side of the arch. The archway had hundreds of little niches and holes and burrows. Another day, Dante might be curious about the odd architecture, but he had a madwoman with a gun chasing him. The arched tunnel was big enough that two semi-trucks could've passed each other. Ahead, thick vegetation and trees grew, and animals cried. Determined to find cover in the trees, Dante sprinted even though every breath made his lungs burn, and his legs wobbled like a new-born colt's. Once clear of the arch, Dante raced across a thick meadow of knee-high grass that gripped his ankles and threatened to trip him.

"You defile the gods," Alb cried out behind him. It was so nice of her to announce her villainy in such unambiguous terms. Dante hoped the Kowri had cameras so the other exalteds realized she was crazy. Then again, if they had cameras, they might've recorded him threatening to burn the temple.

Dante reached the first tree and threw himself into the shadows of roots that rose high above the grass. He didn't have the strength for one more step. He had to hope that Alb raced past him. Dante laid in the dirt and gasped for air quietly.

Seconds later, Alb cleared the arched tunnel and searched the garden.

"Regi claimed that you were respectful. He claimed outsiders could be respectful. And yet here you are, defiling our temple! Outsiders have never offered the Kowri anything but betrayal and lies. I know each story, each example of outsider betrayal." Alb stalked closer, scanning the ground. Dante hoped that she would be as blind as the average greenhorn from Austin. Unfortunately, she spotted the trail he had left through the thick grass and started following it.

Dante crawled backwards through the dirt to put more distance between him and the mad woman. Peaches clung to his back, utterly silent.

"The gods should not allow any life in this universe other than Kowri," Alb said as she advanced on him. Dante didn't have the strength to run anymore. His legs hurt, and he was weak after months of being on a ship. He decided to let his mouth try to slow her down. Using tree branches to climb to his feet, he continued his steady retreat while he called out to her. "It seems like the Lady Divashi is the one who chose to bring us here. That means your gods are on our side not yours."

"Divashi wished to bring her sacred creatures home. Outsiders stole them away, imprisoned them and used them to produce poison that they sell to their own people. That is the sort of depravity that outsiders indulge in. But you appear with a dop so traumatized that she clings to the only creature to offer some succor, and you confuse the others. They don't see that your people are as corrupt as the other outsiders."

"You're not wrong, but your people aren't perfect, either. You're trying to kill people that you agreed to help. I'm fairly sure that makes you a backstabbing asshole."

As Dante hoped, Alb slowed, eager to monologue her villainess beliefs now she had her victim pinned down. Dante would feel better about that if he were not pinned. If this were step one in a trap, he would be feeling smug. But she held the weapon and advanced on him.

"I'm protecting my people from outsiders. They are the plague of every story in which they appear." She sounded unhinged.

"Maybe you only have negative stories about outsiders because the only ones who hang around the borders of your Empire are ones seeking profit. Good people with quiet lives want to avoid you."

"All outsiders are stained with greed." Alb continued her steady advance. The bushes were becoming thicker and starting to impede Dante's retreat.

"You have Gavd ships to investigate crime, so I suspect your people are infected with greed too. From the time that two cells met in a pond and one tried to swallow the other, greed was the defining characteristic of surviving."

"That is the sort of assumption that an outsider would make. Kowri excised the infection of greed. We exiled diseased ones or ensured they cannot corrupt others. Outsiders allow corruption to thrive."

Dante didn't know much about the universe in general, but he couldn't exactly refute her point when it came to humanity. Even when the Supreme Court sided with individual rights, states like Texas transferred authority to private religious institutions so they could continue discriminating. Too many of those people, like his father, did that not because of any philosophical belief or religious tenant but because of greed. Siding with religious separatists gave his father political power, like supporting the Mars colony did.

Every move he made was to gather more and more power. But that wasn't all humans or even most of them, and Dante refused to believe the universe was more corrupt than Earth, not when there were good people like Vk and Ter and Bevit and Ean. And sure, he avoided Ean, but she never held it against the crew that none of them wanted to speak with the ship's psychologist.

"Where are the followers of Gavd that Regi called? Did you kill them?"

She laughed and stopped to hold a low hanging branch. Maybe this slow pursuit through the woods was tiring her. Dante had a small flicker of hope that he might survive this yet. "I would never harm a true Kowri. I am an exalted. When I told them I had plans to deal with Siger and his compatriots, they ceded the field to me because I am a leader here. Regi a'Poque is a traitor who walked away from his people. Poque. The Lady of wanderers. That is the life he wanted, and the life he chose. He cannot now come back and claim the mantle of exalted."

"Lady Divashi settled that one already," Dante pointed out. He had always assumed that if religion were based on cold facts that people would be more rational, but Kowri based their religion off energy readings and documented behaviors from their divine beings, and Alb was still seven pounds of crazy in a five-pound bag.

"Divashi is the Lady of assassination. She heralds the arrival of chaos and disorder. She invites disaster into the Empire. Like you, Regi must go. Her connection to the Empire must be severed."

Dante frowned as creatures stirred behind Alb. "I'm pretty sure you don't get to tell the Lady Divashi what to do," he said.

"I am an exalted of Oba. I am a keeper of stories. I see the prodigious danger laid out in front of us, and I will not leave my people vulnerable to the machinations of a god who embraces disorder and outsiders who have no respect." Her voice rose to a shout.

Dante watched as the trap closed around Alb. "I don't think badmouthing the Lady Divashi is wise." Given that Dante had recently threatened the cold-weather gods, he also suspected himself of rampant stupidity, but hopefully the gods would be a little more forgiving of him because it was clear they were done with Alb.

"What do you know of our gods, outsider?" Alb demanded.

"I know that they take a much more active role in smacking down idiots than my gods," Dante said. "In fact, you might want to look behind you."

Alb glanced behind, her gaze remaining at eye level before she whirled as though expecting Dante to jump out at her. As tired as he was, Dante was certain that if he tried jumping at anyone, he would fall on his face and get shot in the back of the head. Alb then looked down.

Dozens of dops trundled forward, their little round bodies waddling in a way that belied the danger in their quills. Alb retreated. "No. No, I am doing the work of the gods." She brought the weapon up as though she might fire on the dops, and Dante feared he would have to tackle her. Or at least try. However, on her next backward step, she cried out and collapsed in pain as she grabbed her lower leg. "No!"

Dante darted forward, his gaze locked on the weapon, which he grabbed and tossed to one side. Maybe he'd seen too many police movies, but someone grabbing a gun and firing at the last minute was far too common a trope for him to trust a weapon near an enemy, even one that had fallen to the ground. Only then did Dante focus on Alb and realize that Peaches no longer clung to his shirt. She stood beside Alb, her tail up in an attack position and enough quills missing that her rounded tail appeared anorexic. Alb carefully pulled her pant leg away from her skin to show a half dozen barbs sunk deep into the flesh.

"Do your people have medicine for that?" Dante asked. "Where can I go to get you medical help?"

"This is your fault," she said. "You brought this conflict. The other gods are on my side."

Dante considered the way the saber-tooth bear and the pebafri and dops and even the damn pterodactyl things had all defended Regi and Dante. "I'm fairly sure your gods are united. They're united against you."

Alb gasped, her breath rattling. Dante knew there was no help to be found behind the temple. At best, Regi was there unarmed and suffering the aftereffects of his fight with Alb's henchmen. At worst, Regi was dead, and the henchmen were waiting to shoot Dante. So instead, Dante scooped up Peaches. Before he could take a step, the saber-tooth bear thing sprinted into the temple, the ground shaking under his enormous feet. Alb had time to scream once and then the creature had torn her literally in half.

Dante backed away, horrified at the carnage. It was one thing to fantasize about killing someone, but it was quite another to see a person's intestines strung out in the grass.

Chapter Seventeen

Dante stoked Peaches' quills, helping her settle. It hurt to throw so many quills at once, and Peaches was still restless. He wished they could go back to the ship so he and Peaches could hide in their room. They could let Regi in since he was even more bedraggled than Peaches, but Dante wanted to shut out the rest of the world. Unfortunately, a crowd of exalteds had gathered in the garden—clustering around Dante, and Alb's body parts. Someone should carry them off.

"We had no choice," Regi said firmly. He had all four thumbs tucked into his waistband and the fur along his shoulders was standing on end. That probably indicated that he was about ready to throw himself into battle, so Dante didn't mention that it made him fuzzy and cute.

"There is always a choice," Dwill a'Itzpach snapped, his fur equally fuzzy, although he was too brutish to ever look cute. His arms and shoulders were covered with tiny scars that made the hair go in random directions, so that didn't improve his appearance.

"You are young enough to believe that foolishness," Sibja countered. Dante knew she had always supported them, but then Alb had always presented herself as a supporter, and that was making Dante more jaded than normal.

"Outsiders shouldn't even be in the temple," Leevshi said. Like Dwill, he was young.

Dante was starting to recognize the more rounded features of the younger Kowri. Of course, that meant that Regi was on the younger side himself, although he had a much squarer jaw that either Leevshi or Dwill. Dante hoped it was a good sign that it was only the younger exalteds who spoke against them after hearing Regi's story of the fight. It turned out they were Siger's followers, and Alb had manipulated their beliefs because as a follower of Oba, she had collected their stories about their monotheism.

Siger talked. A lot. Apparently when faced with real followers of Gavd, he folded like a cheap paper fan.

Bekdi a'Gavd stepped forward, his huge frame dominating everyone's attention. "The punishment for an outsider violating the temple grounds is clear. The outsider must be executed." The gathering fell silent, not even a rustling foot or stray animal cry breaking the silence.

After several heartbeats' time, Regi threw himself in front of Dante, and Peaches fluffed her quills so fast that Dante damn near carried out that sentence by impaling his hand on her quills.

Nawr a'Ectipic stepped to Bekdi's side. He kept one hand on his walker, and he rested the other on Bekdi's forearm. "We must seek the will of the gods. Our rules are secondary to the will of the gods and only exist if they serve to further the gods' agenda."

"And the gods have made their will clear." A new exalted stepped forward. She was taller than any of the other females and had a stronger color contrast; however, she had the sharper chin and chest of a female.

"The gods have decreed that outsiders will not step foot in a temple." Bekdi narrowed his eyes.

"They have decreed that all outsiders we met before Dante a'Texas must remain outside. However, you are a follower of justice. In interpretations of laws, you should seek guidance of Onidba."

Onidba. The god of logic. He had one follower in town, Gimi a'Onidba. Regi had said that the other two ladies didn't want Gimi to speak for them because her love of logic and counterarguments sometimes confused the issue more than clarifying it, but it looked as if Gimi planned to get involved now. She considered the crowd.

"True or false—disaster is the first blessing of the gods?" she asked. The gathered crowd remained silent for several seconds before Regi answered.

"True."

Gimi nodded. "True or false—Regi a'Divashi and Dante a'Texas requested a ride from a Gavd monotheist?"

Regi glanced at Dante. More than anything, Dante wanted to stay out of this discussion, but he cleared his throat and said, "True."

Gimi smiled at him, a tightening of the face Dante had come to recognize. "True or false, both of you rode and were thrown off a pebafri named after Divashi?"

"True," Regi said. Dante had been more than shocked when he'd learned that tidbit.

Gimi considered the gathered crowd. "That is disastrous. Combined with an intermittent failure in the communication network, I maintain there is enough disaster gathered in one place to conclude the gods have intervened."

"That is conjecture," Bekdi said. He was shaping up to be their biggest opposition, and the head honcho of this whole thing—Nawr—remained silent.

Gimi pursed her lips. "Conjecture supported by god-particles on the communication equipment. That is less conjecture and more logical conclusion. And since I am the exalted of Onidba, determining the logic of the situation is my purview. If I need someone to seek out the thief who continues to sneak into Vroen's orchards to strip his trees of fruit, I will seek your advice." Her words made Bekdi hiss and draw back a step. A whole lot of people then focused their gaze anywhere other than Gimi and Bekdi.

Nawr cleared his throat and leaned on his walker. "We must not take any action that cannot be reversed."

Some of the knots in Dante's stomach loosened as he realized he was not about to be executed.

"What is the oldest and most respected way of determining if an individual is either god-touched or exalted?" Gimi asked.

"No," Nawr said. "We will not have this discussion now."

Gimi raised her arms and moved in a circle to encompass everyone gathered in the garden clearing. "We have enough exalteds from all three temples here to make decisions. Logic demands that we seek truth, no matter how uncomfortable, but Nawr, you seek to protect us from an uncomfortable truth. While that is fitting for one who follows the Lady Ectipic, I am of the Lord Onidba and I will not turn my head from truth."

"We are not denying truth," someone called from the back.

"Reui a'Rvion," Regi whispered. While Dante appreciated the information, he didn't recognize either name. The Kowri had too many gods to remember them all, and Reui hadn't featured in any of the stories Regi had brought back to the ship about the debates over how to handle a ship of outsiders.

"You are," Gimi said firmly. "Otherwise you would see that Dante a'Texas was first presented disaster and then opportunity. And if Kowri eyes insist on being blind, the Lady Divashi then guided her own creatures to be Alb's executioners. And the one god none of us dare challenge then sent his sacred beast to finish her."

"Not every action of a sacred creature is the will of a god. They still eat and shit," another called. Regi didn't provide a name this time, so perhaps he didn't recognize everyone here either. That made sense because there were a lot of people in the garden. The grass and bushes were getting trampled.

"And a freio provided cover and prevented Dante a'Texas from rushing into battle unarmed."

At Gimi's words, Bekdi crossed his arms in a gesture so human that Dante could almost see his own father superimposed over the Kowri man. "By that measure, the gods do not love Regi a'Divashi because they allowed him to enter that same battle unarmed."

Gimi sniffed. "Perhaps they have more need of Dante. Perhaps they have more faith in Regi's training. I do not pretend to know the gods' minds. I only know a freio protected Dante a'Texas until he had the opportunity to enter the temple. And the acceptance of temple animals within the temple proper is the ultimate test of who is exalted. Disaster, opportunity, and the acceptance of temple animals—the signs are clear. If you add a respectable layer of fur and additional thumbs to Dante, we would all welcome him to the status of exalted."

Bekdi stood straighter, and several Kowri backed away as though Dante had the plague.

Dante stroked Peaches. He now understood why people might want to prevent Gimi from speaking in their favor. She made people uncomfortable. "Maybe that's taking a little far. I might limit it to saying your gods and I have mutual friends that we want to protect."

Gimi stepped up to Regi, so close that their chests almost touched. "If I asked you to walk up to the freio, would you have any reservations?" She nodded toward where the saber-tooth bear thing stood eating the hindquarter of a large animal. Dante hoped that was something one of the temple workers had given him and not another sacred animal. Sadly, it might have been the rear leg of the old pebafri that Regi had been forced to put down after he'd won his fight. While irrational, Dante was angrier about that animal's death than he was the deaths of Siger's pals. They deserved it, but the gods were assholes for not protecting that pebafri.

"Sacred animals are safe. I already stumbled and fell into him once, so I don't have a problem with him."

Gimi whirled on Bekdi. "Are you equally sanguine about approaching a freio?"

Bekdi hesitated long enough to make his real answer known, but he drew himself up to his full height. "Of course I am. I am an exalted." He strode over toward the creature. He was six or seven feet away when the freio bit down on the thigh bone hard enough that it broke with a thunderous crack. Bekdi jumped, but to his credit, he continued walking to the beast, stopping a few inches from it. The freio gave him an unimpressed look and walked away, his dinner in his mouth.

"I would urinate on myself before doing that," Gimi said. "Yet that freio protected Dante a'Texas because Lord Retav himself wished to make himself clear. Do any of you wish to contradict the Lord of retribution? Is there another reason for the freio to be here rather than the harvest-season temple where he is our most sacred and most dangerous animal?"

"You cannot possibly give an outsider the title of exalted."

"I am an exalted of Onidba. The thing I cannot do is dismiss logic." With that, she walked away.

Sibja sighed. "She is a difficult woman. Debates in the harvest-season temple do tend to end with her bludgeoning us with logic until we admit that she is right. However, she has a point. How many years has it been since a freio has attended the temple? The fact that he came to the wrong temple does suggest that the gods have made their point clear."

Nawr winced. "I believe we should all separate and think about the issues Gimi a'Onidba has presented." He started across the open field, his powered walker bumping across the uneven ground.

"Outsiders are not allowed in the temple," Bekdi repeated himself. Dante imagined the man wanted to stomp his feet, but most of the other exalteds avoided his gaze, and a few even gave Dante careful smiles. Regi stepped back until he pressed his shoulder into Dante's.

"I think you earned a promotion."

"I don't want one," Dante whispered back.

"I didn't either." Regi limped toward the front of the temple. Clumps of bloody fur decorated the right side of his face and he seemed to have hurt his left leg. Dante hurried after him, sliding an arm around Regi's waist and taking some of his weight. For a second, Regi studied him. But then he slung an arm over Dante's shoulders. They made their way toward the front of the temple and Dante hoped they had medical care on the way. Regi had taken a lot of blows. He also hoped the gods left them alone for a while. If either of them had any more of the gods' first blessing, they might end up dead.

Hell, Dante was surprised they weren't dead already.

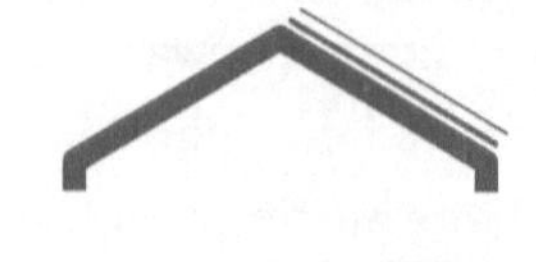

Chapter Eighteen

"They should have given you medical care in town," Bevit gave a head jerk that spoke of her disapproval of Kowri medical services. Regi would rather avoid her judgment, but his injuries required treatment, and he felt safer with Bevit than he did with the temple exalteds.

"They offered treatment, but I preferred your skills." Regi gave her his best smile.

A wrinkle formed between her eyes. "I have raised four children, and each had mastered disingenuous compliments better than that before they turned ten."

Dante snorted.

Bevit pointed her two forward-facing fingers at him. "You took several falls and were involved in a dangerous chase despite the weakness in your breathing structures. You will submit to an exam next."

Dante froze, his eyes wide.

Captain Cota stepped forward, commanding everyone's attention. "I am still confused about why the debate appears to have shifted focus to Dante." His gaze flicked in his direction. Regi would have assumed the captain was relaxed except he had tangled his long fingers into a complex knot. He was upset, but given the situation, the concern was reasonable.

"The temple no longer has any interest in debating whether the crew should be eliminated," Regi pointed out. That was a positive outcome—a far better one than Regi had expected when he'd woken this morning. Divashi had given them so much luck they had nearly died of it, but he and Dante had come through with only minor injuries. Regi counted that a win.

"Now they are trying to decide if they have to listen to me as some sort of leader," Dante said. "News. They should not. Before the slavers took me off Earth, I had trouble running my own life. I certainly couldn't be trusted to make decisions for anyone else."

"An exalted is supposed to follow the guidance of the gods, not have answers at the ready," Regi said. Both Cota and Bevit tensed. The heart monitor flashed faster as Regi's blood pressure rose. He hated the way the others could dismiss the existence of Kowri gods even when the evidence was in front of them.

"It's hard to ignore the guidance when we were practically shoved head-first into the back of the temple. I don't know whether your gods are literal gods or not, but they are incredibly powerful, incredibly unsubtle creatures." Dante looked at the ceiling and addressed Divashi in impious tones. "I'm still cranky about the kidnapping plot. Both plots. You can stop letting people grab me because it makes me unhappy."

Bevit and Cota both considered Dante with concern.

"What?" he asked.

Cota and Bevit exchanged glances full of meaning.

"Seriously," Dante said, "I get that you don't want to believe in gods, so don't. But if you can't see that the Kowri live with a very powerful co-species or non-corporeal partners or something, then you're both some shade of stupid."

Regi coughed loudly. Cota's pupils had narrowed to slits, but Bevit appeared amused. "So," she asked, "will they let us leave soon? This planet was beautiful from space, but even a cramped space station is better than paradise if you aren't allowed out of the ship."

"Most likely," Regi said. Dante was now cooing at Peaches. The dop had helped to kill an exalted, but Dante still considered her fondly. Dante might not believe the gods were actual gods, but he put his faith in them to an extent Regi wasn't used to seeing, even in Kowri. The last person who had this much faith in the gods was his mother. That was an uncomfortable thought. "Dante might not have intended to challenge at the temple, but the fact remains that he passed a temple challenge and with so many sacred animals presenting at the temples, none of the exalteds wish to question the will of the gods."

"I care less about internal Kowri politics than I do getting our crew home," Cota said. "What can I do to ensure that? I had meetings set up, but I have received word that all of them have been cancelled."

"They want me off their planet, don't they?" Dante appeared oddly delighted by the idea.

"They do," Regi agreed. "And since the Coalition ship is here and willing to take you out of the Empire, that seems the most likely course of action."

"Could we get permission to leave soon?"

"It could be imminent," Regi said. If he knew his people, their inability to fit Dante into their construct of the universe would make them invite him to leave as soon as possible.

"I should talk to Ter," Cota said. "I still wish I could have spoken to some of the exalteds but given a choice of making history with the Empire or getting the crew out without any casualties, I think I prefer the second." Cota abandoned the small infirmary in haste.

Bevit's strip of quill-like hair shivered the way Peaches sometimes shook her quills. "I should catch up on my reports. When I thought we might not be allowed to return to Coalition space, I took that as permission to neglect my accounts." Given that Efhtee had an almost religious belief in avoiding boredom, that didn't surprise Regi.

"I hope Vk has completed ours," Regi said. Like Bevit he had neglected his report writing to an unforgivable extent. "I should check."

"No!" Bevit said sharply. "You have a head injury, and the brain is not an organ we can regenerate. You will sit in a semi-dark room and do something that involves quiet contemplation and no reading. And you may not be alone."

"I can sit with him," Dante offered.

Bevit huffed. For long seconds, she studied him as if judging his trustworthiness with a patient. Over half the exalteds believed or at least suspected Dante spoke for the gods, but Bevit was more exacting when it came to her patients than Kowri were with their chosen exalteds. "If he acts odd, you need to call me."

Dante nodded.

"If he tries reading or writing reports you need to call me."

Dante held his hand up, his fingers arranged oddly. "Scout's honor," he said. Regi and Bevit both frowned as the translation failed. "I will," Dante amended himself.

"If he tries to arrest any crew, trip him and then sit on him," Bevit ordered.

Dante gave Regi a wide grin that showed so many teeth that Regi thought of a predator about to pounce on its dinner. "I can do that."

Bevit huffed. "Regi, wear the monitor, but you can go with Dante." With that, she retreated into her office.

"Your place or mine?" Dante asked. From the tone, Regi suspected the phrase had some cultural significance, but he couldn't identify it, so he chose to take it at face value.

"My place has fewer dop droppings."

"True." Dante came to the side of the bed and hovered as Regi got to his feet. For a medically fragile species, he had more strength than Regi had anticipated. On the walk across the temple, he had learned to trust Dante to support his weight, so Regi put an arm across Dante's shoulders.

"I might have delicious contraband that has not found its way to the proper incineration protocol." Regi had never offered to share his confiscated contraband before, but Dante was a special case.

"That sounds like a date," Dante said.

The translation offered a rush of ideas associated with "date," but since Regi didn't disagree with any of them, he cooperated as Dante helped him to the infirmary door. He might not understand "date," but he knew he did like to spend time with Dante. Since they were both now confirmed to be cursed with the attention of a capricious god, it was important that they support one another. If that required more time together hiding in some converted space and sharing contraband sweets and intoxicants, Regi was willing to make that sacrifice.

Author's Note

It has been a joy to head back into space. Regi and Dante are part of a very different universe than my other science fiction, but there is something very familiar about coming home to "the black" between the stars. As always, I owe some much to the Patreon readers who support me during the dry spells between publications. I need to call out a special thanks for Angel, Annie, Atheistic Snail, Beth, Carolyn, Catherine, Emma, Jeanette, Saharra Shadow, Sarah, SG, Sheena, Zil, Aiisha, Alyssa, Amber, Angelica, Anja, Aude, Brigette, Carlene, Caroline, Colby, Elizabeth (and the other Elizabeth, and the other, other Elizabeth), Elyssa, Gemma, Hollye, Janelle, Jean, Jeff, Jennifer (and the other Jennifer), Jennskifer, Jess, Jill, Judith, Julia, Julie, Karen, Kay, Kimi, L, Leah, Lisa, Mandy, Marnie, Martina, Mary, Megan, Michele, Nanette, Ninna, Odessa, Pen, Philippa, Pim, Rebecca, Rnngwen, Sarah, Sasha, Simone, Suzu, Taya, Thothkristen, Tor, and Victoria. In particular, I have to thank Sarah, who absolutely refused to let me give up, even when the depression monster was gnawing on my bones. A lot. It has done a lot of gnawing lately.